# JAY

# Other Novels by W. Royce Adams

*Me & Jay*

*The Computer's Nerd*

*Rairarubia*
*Return to Rairarubia*
*Raid on Rairarubia*
*Revenge on Rairarubia*
*Ring from Rairarubia*

# JAY

W. Royce Adams

A sequel to *Me & Jay*

**Unlimited Publishing**
Bloomington, Indiana

**Rairarubia Books**
Santa Barbara, California

Copyright © 2005 by W. Royce Adams

Distributing Publisher:
Unlimited Publishing LLC
Bloomington, Indiana

Contributing Publisher:
Rairarubia Books
Santa Barbara, California

http://www.unlimitedpublishing.com

LCCN: 2004117919

First edition.

Copies of this fine book and others
are available to order online at:

http://www.unlimitedpublishing.com/authors

ISBN 1-58832-120-7

Cataloging Data:

Jay / by W. Royce Adams—1st ed.
Summary: When 16 year-old Jay Thornton's mother dies leaving him an orphan, he jumps a freight train to get away from being placed in a foster home and discovers an unexpectedly dangerous lifestyle.

LCCN: 2004117919
ISBN: 1-58832-120-7

1. Runaway teenagers—Juvenile fiction. 2. Orphans—Juvenile fiction.
3. Tramps—Juvenile fiction. 4. New Age persons—Juvenile fiction.

[1. Runaways—Fiction. 2. Orphans—Fiction. 3. Tramps—Fiction.
4. New Age Persons—Fiction. 5. Railroads—Fiction. 6. Orphan Train—Fiction.]

[Fic]
QBI 04-700509

Rairarubia Books
Santa Barbara, California

Unlimited Publishing
Bloomington, Indiana

# Acknowledgements

Credit and appreciation go to Jane Brody, Kate Brody-Adams, and editors Sharon Dirlam and John McCafferty for their sound advice and helpful suggestions in writing this sequel to *Me & Jay*.

# Foreword

While all the characters in *Jay* are fictitious, some of the names of people referred to in the story are real and used for effect. In doing research for this story, I discovered numerous books and web links to information about past and present freight-train riders. I read about "Children of the Rails," orphans who were shipped out west to rid New York of thousands of street urchins. I found original stories of the hardships suffered by many forced to jump trains to find work during the depression in the mid-1900s. I learned that yearly hobo meetings are held to elect the King and Queen of the Hobos. Steam Train Maury Graham, elected King five times, wrote a book about his rail-riding experiences. Even now, a group calling themselves "The Hobohemians" uses cell phones and the Internet to plan their illegal train catching.

Like the character Jay in this novel, a growing number of young fright-train riders put their lives in danger daily. Homeless for whatever reason, they hangout wherever they can "catch out" aboard a freight that takes them no place in particular. Living on handouts or diving into garbage bins to eat, bumming for change, and sometimes stealing, these young "new-age hobos" are part of a growing band of train hoppers. What may seem like a fun, adventurous, even romantic life is in reality anything but. Hundreds of train jumpers die or are arrested every year. It is not only illegal, but perilous.

I know firsthand. I still bear a scar on my side from a stupid escapade with "catching out."

*The story you are about to read takes place two years after the end of Me & Jay . . .*

# CHAPTER 1

T HEY CAUGHT SEVEN of us jumping off the boxcar when the train pulled in. I don't know how they knew it, but as soon as our feet hit the gravel, strong flashlight beams hit us in the face. Scared and nervous, I couldn't tell who they were or how many there were. Shouting nasty orders, they force-marched us into an old, windowless railroad shack. Inside, the gloomy yellow lighting and gross, stuffy smell gave my stomach an uneasy turn. What had I gotten myself into?

I noticed they didn't wear uniforms or show us any badges. But right then none of us doubted they were the law. The guns pointed at us were proof enough. I'd heard stories, mostly not good, about railroad cops—"bulls," they call them. But this was no story.

I've been afraid big time before, like that time me and Geri—yeah, I know—Geri and I got into that cave trouble, but never like this. On my own now, this was scarier—way scarier. I just prayed my shaky knees wouldn't buckle on me, or worse, my bladder betray me.

You could tell one of the men with a gun was enjoying his catch. With a mean grin, he drawled out, "Now, you ho-bos know you can't ride the railroad without a ticket. Any of you 'bos got a ticket?"

He knew we didn't. Just yankin' us around. He shook his head and waved his gun, meaning he wanted us to line up. Another guy in the shadows kept smacking a long, black club against his thigh. "You deadbeats ought to know the routine by now. Against the wall." He held a big flashlight in the other hand and kept pointing the beam into each of our faces.

We all backed up against the wall, shoulder to shoulder. I didn't know anyone in the lineup. I'd only been riding the freight for about two hours when the train stopped here—wherever here was. When I'd jumped on I noticed there were some others in the car, but nobody spoke, which suited me fine.

"Now strip."

I didn't think I'd heard right. But the men on either side of me started grumbling and taking off their clothes like they'd lived through this before. Someone started to protest, but he got the end of a club rammed into his stomach. He went down, gasping, trying to find air. I gasped myself. I could hear my speeding heart beat in my ears. This wasn't what I'd run away for.

"Any one else here think they're privileged?" the bull yelled. He waved his club and his flashlight all along the row of us. Before the flashlight beam reached me, my all-thumbs fingers went to work undressing.

We stood there with all our clothes and whatever packs we carried at our feet. Embarrassed, I felt totally helpless fidgeting there naked, worried stiff what might happen next. Another man appeared from nowhere. He started going through our stuff. No sleeping bag, backpack or pocket got left out. The brims of hats, insides of shoes, and even belts got checked. Every time money was found, which wasn't often, it was handed to one of the guys with a gun.

By the time the railroad cop reached my stuff, they'd only collected a few dollars and let us know they weren't too happy about it. I had a twenty, which I thought I'd hidden pretty well in the lining of my jacket. But this guy found it almost like he knew where it was. He looked at me, held the twenty in my face, smiled, then handed it to the other guy. Then he shook out my sleeping bag, went through the pockets of both pairs of jeans, shook out my two shirts, even checked in my rolled-up spare socks and shorts. The photo of my mom fell to the floor and I reached for it.

Before I could get it, he smacked my arm. "Watch it! Stand back," he barked. He gave me a look, picked up the photo, looked, and threw it on the floor again. He tossed aside what little food I had, but took the last of my cigarettes, found my Swiss Army knife and slipped it into his pocket. The guy was an expert on searching. I don't know where I could have hidden anything without it being found. Mostly, I hated to lose my knife, but standing around buck-naked shivering, scared about what could happen next, bothered me a big bunch more.

The collector continued down the line until everything had been searched and all the money found. He nodded to the one with the club.

The one with the club started walking down the line. He tapped his club on the shoulder of the first guy in line, still holding his stomach and wheezing, and said, "You stay." He tapped the next man's shoulder. "Get dressed." The next was told to stay.

When he got to me, he tapped me and said, "You stay."

My knees almost folded, and I came close to letting my bladder speak for my fear.

The collector spoke up. "Naw, that one had money. He can get dressed."

I felt the flashlight beam search up and down my naked body.

"Why, he's just a kid," the bull said. "Tall for your age, ain'tcha. How old are you, boy? Fifteen? Sixteen?" He laughed. "You don't even have a good patch of hair between your skinny legs yet." He held his light on me there. I tried to cover myself with my hands. Most helpless, useless, upsetting feeling in the world, for sure.

I didn't know if he really wanted me to answer or not. But I couldn't form a word in my dry mouth if I tried. He smiled, seeing me shaking, mostly from fear, but now from some anger, too, especially with everybody laughing at my expense. Even some of the riders joined in. I felt my face turn hot. Yeah, real funny, you bunch of . . .

Right then, I wanted to gain ten years and twenty pounds. I'd laugh while I used his stupid club on him. All of them.

He grinned at me. "What's your name, little 'bo?"

I ran my tongue around my teeth, trying to wet my dry mouth. I managed to get out a weak. "Jay."

"What say?" He bent his ear toward me like he hadn't heard. He had.

I forced out another "Jay," a little louder.

"Jay, huh? A runaway, I bet. Shall we turn him in? Maybe there's a *re*-ward." He held the light right on my face.

I had to close my eyes and turn my head.

"Fat chance of that," the man with the gun said. "Look at him. Who'd want him?"

More laughter.

"Well, runaway Jay, get dressed, then. But try to find yourself some better company than these here railroad trespassers. Consider yourself lucky this time."

When he moved to the next one in line, I wasted no time getting my clothes on, though I didn't know what to expect next. Were they going to take us to jail? I for sure didn't want them to send me back to Allonia. Did they have a reward out for me?

"Now listen up," the main cop said. "The railroad doesn't run a charity train. It needs to be paid for its services. There's forty-one dollars and some change collected here." He held up the money. "We figure the fare for the last ride comes to ten dollars and fifty cents each. Since you so willingly and graciously pooled your funds for us, there's enough here to cover the fares for the four of you who paid."

Yeah, like the money was going to the railroad. They stole my money and my knife! These guys were thieves!

He put the money in his pocket. "Now beat it, and don't let us catch you again. The railroad has passenger trains if you want to travel. This here town don't cotton to deadbeats. Put that in your memory bank."

Still mad about losing my stuff, it took me a minute before I realized I was free to go. The dressed hobos—that's what I'd become—a hobo—beat it out the door. Shoes unlaced, I shoved my stuff in my pack and took off, worried they'd stop me at the door or do something bad.

I heard some protests coming from the ones left behind, then some whacks and pain-like yelling, but I wasn't about to hang around to find out what I imagined was happening to them.

I just took off running fast as I could with untied shoes and a pack. A couple of times I almost tripped in the dark over all the tracks. I didn't see where the other three went and didn't care. No bond held us together. I was alone. A loner.

Like the bull said, "Runaway Jay."

So I ran.

# CHAPTER 2

I STOPPED RUNNING when I felt far enough away from the train shack. I ducked between two dark buildings and relieved myself before I really lost control. My sweaty shirt stuck to my back and I got a whiff of what I smelled like. A mixture of stink picked up from three days of rail traveling in different dirty boxcars.

I slumped down against a wall and sat on my pack. My heart still pumped in overtime. My hands shook so bad I had trouble tying my boots. I caught my body rocking back and forth and told myself to calm down.

I couldn't. I keep thinking about what happened, telling myself it could have been worse. Like, what if they'd made me stay? Sure, they took my money and my knife, but they let me go. I tried not to think about how it might have been worse, about my anger at those men, my embarrassment.

Except I did think about it, and it caused me to let my guard down. The more I tried to stop the tears, the more choked up I got. Thankfully, I hadn't broken down earlier in front of everybody. But right then, every bad thing in my life caught up with me.

I told myself to go ahead. Get it all out. Then never cry again. Never. I cried when mom died, and I allowed myself that cry. But that was it. Nobody made me run away. Being on the road was all my doing. I chose to take off. I made the decision, and now I had to take responsibility for my actions. I wasn't about to let them put me in no foster home. No way. Geri and Randall hadn't understood when I told them. I thought they might since they knew me better than anybody. But with mom gone, I had to split.

When the tears stopped, I searched through my stuff and found mom's picture. I couldn't really see it in the dark, but I knew it by heart. I ran my finger over it. They say I look like her—tall, same straight nose, blue-green eyes, hair black as ink, pretty shaggy right now. For a moment, I got mad at her. Why'd see go and die on me? The doctor warned her about smoking. Why didn't she listen? First dad, when I was younger, now mom. What was I supposed to do? No relatives, I felt like the world wanted me out of the way.

Quit whining, I told myself. I'll make it. I have to. Tonight put one of those life calluses you get that helps make you a survivor. I intend to be one of the survivors of the fittest.

"I'll be okay, mom," I promised her, as I put her picture away.

Okay, enough. What next? Where to go? Stay in the rail yard and hop another train? Those yahoos might catch me again. The thought kept me from getting up. But I had to do something.

A train horn blasted three times off to my left and I jumped. I told myself to relax. Maybe the train was leaving and could get me away from here. Maybe I could hop it while the bulls were busy in the shack. I couldn't think of a better plan. What choice did I have, anyway? I couldn't just sit in the dark with no money or food forever.

My legs still shaking, I sneaked off toward the sound of the train, hiding in the shadows as best I could.

The train yard was pretty empty, just some cars sitting on the side. Another blast from the diesel's horn and I spotted it. A freight was backing up and I heard the domino clacking sound of the car couplings connecting. Then the train shuddered and strained forward. It hadn't picked up speed yet. No bulls around that I could see. No boxcars with doors open either. But I saw a flatcar with not much on it, something covered over by a big tarp on one end.

I ran alongside, threw my pack up, grabbed on to the ladder and swung myself up on the platform. I didn't know where I was or where I was going. I didn't care. I needed to get away from what I'd just been through.

Stretched out on my back, I looked up at the stars for a while. Lay low, I figured, until the train picked up speed and left the town that hates hobos.

Just when I thought I was free, the metal wheels screeched to a stop. I sat up, thinking that I'd been spotted and they'd found me out. But the train shuddered and jerked into motion again, in the other direction. Once we were moving, I got on my hands and knees and looked around. I decided to move closer to whatever it was tied down under the heavy tarp. The flatcar wobbled, making it hard to crawl along.

When I got to the tarp, I lifted a corner. Too dark to tell what it was. Probably some kind of engine or machinery, I guessed from the heavy oily smell. The tarp would make a good cover come daylight, so I shoved my pack under and sat there watching the shadows of trees and buildings speed by until we were out in open country.

I really wanted to smoke and hoped the guy who stole my cigarettes got lung cancer like my mom. Ah, well, Geri's been after me to quit anyway. You'd think I might learn something from my mom's bad habit.

I thought back about the time I tried to show Geri how to smoke and we ended up starting a grass fire that almost made us toast. That was after we'd hopped a freight to go up the river road. I remember telling her how I would like to have been a hobo during the depression in the 1930s. Now, here I was.

But not as sure anymore.

Thinking about Geri made me picture Randall and his backyard tire swing. We had some fun there. I felt sorry now that I used to give him a bad time about correcting my English and stuff. I guess it annoyed me he's the smarter one. I took advantage of the guy trying to be a friend. Geri and I still owed him for his canteen we lost on our little cave excursion. Funny thoughts you get when you're heading away from home. I had to fight off that lonesome feeling.

The motion of the train helped and put me to sleep for a bit. When I opened my eyes, the sky was getting brighter and the stars were gone. It was time to get under the tarp, just in case some bulls were on board. I needed more sleep.

I lifted the heavy tarp and crawled under into the smell of oil and gasoline. I groped around the machinery, searching for a space to stretch out. Not able to see, I reached out in front of me. My hand touched what felt like a leg.

"Let go if you know what's good for ya'."

It *was* a leg.

I let go with a jump and tried to sit up, but the heavy tarp didn't give me much room. I didn't need any more trouble.

"Sorry. Didn't know anyone was under here."

A sudden flashlight beam blinded me for a second. I shielded my face with my hand. Twice in one night was twice too many. Then the light went off.

"Can't be too careful," the voice in the dark said. "You plan to be trouble?"

"No trouble from me," I answered, still not seeing a face.

"Where you headed?" I was asked.

"California, eventually." That's where I thought I wanted to go when I left.

"You'll never make it on this train."

"Yeah? Where's it headed?" At this point I didn't care a whole lot.

"Chicago."

"Guess I'll take the long way around." I tried to sound like I didn't care. But I was heading back the direction I came from. This was the second time I'd grabbed the wrong train. The one I'd been on had come from Chicago headed for East St. Louis. I thought I'd catch something headed west from there. Now I was going backward again.

"Any stops before Chicago?" I asked my still unseen partner. His voice sounded young.

"New at this, huh?" He gave a little laugh I didn't care for. Definitely a young guy.

How'd he know? Well, it was the truth. Why lie? "Yeah. Couple days now."

"See, what you need to do," said the voice in the dark, "is check the train schedules before you grab anything. Unless you really don't care where you end up. Some don't. But that can be dangerous."

"Why? Are schedules posted somewhere?" This was information I definitely could use if I wanted to get to California.

"Sorta. You can check out stuff on the Internet."

"The Internet?" Was he pulling my leg? I doubted train jumpers carried computers around.

"Yeah, e-mail can keep you posted on what train's good to catch and what towns to stay away from. I use library computers mostly, sometimes cyber cafés if I've got the cash. Libraries are usually free."

I didn't know what a cyber café was, so I asked.

The voice laughed at me. "You are a greenie. Anyway, most towns have 'em now. They're places, like coffee shops or bars, places where you can use computers for a fee, go on line, check your e-mail, keep up on all kinds of stuff. I only use 'em if the library in the town I'm in doesn't have an Internet connection. Most do now."

"You can get freight train schedules on line?" I never used a computer at school much, didn't have the patience.

"Mostly it's through e-mail connections with other riders. Some guys have cell phones, others e-mail accounts. They'll call in train movements to friends who post the information on the Internet. That way, we get some idea of what trains are going where. You should fool around with some search engines on the web sometime. You'll find all kinds of helpful stuff."

"Yeah. Thanks." I wasn't sure what a search engine was, but I wasn't about to ask.

"No problem. You got a name?"

"Jay. Jay Thornton." I didn't mean to give my whole name. Just came out.

"That's your real name, right?"

"Yeah. Why?"

"Well, it's a good idea not to give out your real name. 'Specially if you're a runaway. People ask around, ya' know. Eventually they can track you down. You need to make up a rail name."

That made sense. "You gotta rail name?" I asked.

"Liberty Two."

I nodded, wondering why he picked that name when he came right out and told me.

"See, I once heard a guy tell someone he wasn't at liberty to tell his real name. That's my story, too. I'm not at liberty to tell." He laughed. "But since there's already someone I know and respect named Liberty, I call myself Liberty Two."

"That's cool," I told him. I wondered what I should call myself. I didn't want anyone tracking me down. If they even were looking for me. You never know.

"You holdin'?" Liberty Two asked.

"What?" I didn't now what he meant.

"Drugs. You got any weed, horse, meth . . . ?"

"No," I snapped back. I didn't, and I don't do drugs, but I thought it was pretty nosey of him to ask.

"Good. Drugs and catchin' out don't mix. You need to have a clear head to do what we do. Once I saw a stoned idiot try for a grab at a tanker car and he wound up gettin' his leg sliced off."

Neither one of us said anything for a bit. That's when I noticed how hot and bad it smelled under the tarp. I didn't know whether it was him, me, or the thick old oily cover. Kinda toilety rank. Plus, I was getting a cramp in my leg from being bent over under the tarp like a yogi in a yoga pose I couldn't do. But that all left my mind when I felt the train lurch, the iron wheels screech and the couplings clash.

Invisible Liberty Two said, "Oh, oh."

"What?" I didn't like the way he said it.

"We shouldn't be slowin' down. Not yet." He lifted a piece of the tarp to peek out.

It was bright day now and I saw his face for the first time. Liberty Two didn't look much older than me. His dirty blond hair needed a good cutting, peach fuzz on his chin. He dropped the tarp and I was blind again.

"According to the schedule I got, we should be railin' to Springfield, not stoppin'. We couldn't be there yet." He sounded too alarmed to suit me. My first thought was bulls. Did they know we were on the train? Maybe they were going to stop the train and search it. I asked Liberty Two what he thought.

"Somethin's not right. Maybe the train hit somethin'. Maybe it's a bull check. My gut tells me to jump before it stops," he said. "My gut's usually right," he added. He lifted the tarp again, this time throwing it back some so we were both exposed to the rising sun. Keeping low, he crawled to the edge of the flatcar. He looked up ahead and then back down. I don't know what he was looking for.

I stayed low myself and crawled out from under the tarp. All I saw were some trees and a field of wheat. I had no idea were I was, except somewhere in Illinois on my way to Chicago. Runaway-wrong-way Jay.

The train kept slowing.

"Don't know about you, buddy, but I'm playin' it safe and bailin' 'till I can see what's wrong." Liberty Two crawled back to the tarp and grabbed his pack. "Comin'?" he asked and jumped clear. I watched as he ran along and then disappeared.

He knew a lot more about riding freights than I did. And sure as a bee stings I didn't want to face any more railroad cops. So I hooked my arm through a backpack strap, took a deep breath, and jumped.

When I hit the ground, my left ankle didn't cooperate. Pain charged through my body, reminding me it wasn't made for jumping off moving trains. I went down way wrong and way too hard.

# CHAPTER 3

I TUMBLED OVER at least once, maybe twice. My pack saved my head from getting brained on an old railroad tie I fell against. It stopped me cold but not the hurting. I checked out my ankle. It hurt to move it, but it didn't seem broken. I felt lucky I'd just twisted it. Still, it hurt.

I sat there groaning and cussing, when Liberty Two came out of nowhere. I felt like such a stup. He would have to see me like this.

He began to help me up. "Come on. The train's almost stopped. We gotta get outta here in case they're doin' a search."

Liberty Two was taller than me and maybe even skinnier. But he was strong. He half pulled me up and put my arm around his shoulder. He helped me limp away from the train and into a small grove of trees. When I sat down against one, I saw the long train sitting still on the tracks.

Squatting next to me, Liberty Two brushed his long, dirty blond hair from his eyes. "They can't do anything to us here. We're off the railroad's property now."

"Thanks for helping me," I said, trying to ignore the new stings growing from cuts and scratches. I didn't want to look at them in front of Liberty Two. But it wasn't easy.

"No problem. See, I'm a member of H.O.B.O. now," he said with a proud smile that needed a little dental work.

My elbow was killing me, but I wasn't going to look at it. "What's that?"

"Help Our Brothers Overcome. H.O.B.O. It's an organization started by another Liberty. Liberty Justice, King of the Hobos. I just came from a big meeting a few days ago back around Iowa. I joined up."

An hobo organization? Was he pulling my leg? "Didn't know there was such a thing." To heck with it. I checked my bloody elbow. A bad scrape, enough to keep me pissed at myself for not jumping off like a real rail rider.

"Any freight rider can join if you agree with the rules." He started digging around in his backpack. One shoulder strap was missing, so he'd rigged up some kind of rope replacement.

"What rules?"

"Simple. Don't steal anything that's on the trains and don't damage any railroad property." He pulled out a small, once white, dirt-smeared first aid kit and handed it to me.

"Thanks," I said, surprised.

"See, the way Liberty Justice sees it, if the railroads let us ride the trains with no hassle, we agree to keep the faith and stop anyone we see breakin' the rules. There's some gauze and disinfectant in there." He pointed at the box I hadn't opened yet. "You might wanna dump some on that elbow."

I nodded.

He went on once I'd opened the kit. "The way Liberty Justice figures it, we're like going to ride the trains anyway, so why not work somethin' out with 'em. LJ said more and more kids like us are ridin' these days and don't know what we're doin'. Lotta' people gettin' killed and that don't look good for the railroad. Somethin's gotta be done."

Careful not to waste any, I poured some antiseptic stuff on the gauze and placed it on my cut, trying not to wince. "Uh, so, what's the railroad say about this? Last place I was, the bulls weren't about to go along with anything like that." I didn't think those thieves were real bulls, but I tried to sound experienced.

He pulled his knees up and wrapped his arms around his legs. "Nothing official yet. The meeting in Iowa? Some railroad dude actually showed up. He listened, said he'd talk to his boss. Told us that last year, over eight thousand arrests were made for freight-train riding." Liberty Two shrugged.

Eight thousand? I let out a little whistle.

Liberty Two nodded. "So you can imagine how many of us must be ridin' and not getting caught. So, H.O.B.O. could be a start, ya' know? Could work out for both sides."

Not in my lifetime, I thought, but I didn't say anything. My knees stung, so I pulled up my pant legs. Deep scrape, pieces of pant leg and blood. I dabbed the gauze on both knees. "How'd you hear about the meeting? I mean, how do you members keep in touch?" I gave back the first aid kit.

He put it in his pack. "Like I told ya', the Hobo Internet. There's a bunch of us rail riders who have e-mail addresses, either private or through libraries. Liberty Justice gives plenty of notice before each meeting so we can get there in time if we're across country. There's a big meeting every year and we vote for a King of the Hobos."

A king of the hobos? Yeah, maybe in the movies. I couldn't help wonder how much of what he said was true.

I put my pack under my head and stretched out. I could feel my legs stiffening from the cuts.

"No meanness intended, but you're pretty green to be on the rails. If you're really gonna become a hobo, you need to know what you're getting into. It's a tough, lonely life with a lot of dangers you gotta look out for."

"Yeah, I got a little taste of that back down the line," I said, trying not to sound totally green.

"If ya' want, I'll show you how to use the Internet if the next town's got a library hookup." Liberty Two patted up his backpack, placed it under his head and stretched out next to me.

"Yeah, sure." It felt good to just rest my aches.

"Leadin' a hobo's life ain't such a bad life," he said, looking up at the sky. "I do alright."

When I didn't say anything, he went on, "Say, you know where the name 'hobo' came from?" he asked.

I shook my head. He sure liked to talk. I wondered if it had been a while since he'd had anyone who'd listen. I got the feeling he might be lonely. Or maybe setting me up.

"Couple theories about the name. The one that makes the most sense to me goes way back to when guys wanderin' the country lookin' for work put all their stuff in a sack and tied it to a garden hoe. They'd use their hoes to work in fields or on farms to earn meals. They'd hitchhike, jump freights, walk any place they might find work. People called 'em 'hoe-boys.' After awhile the term got shortened to hobos."

"How long you been doin' this?" I asked, cautious about his friendliness.

"Oh, about four years, I guess."

Four years? He couldn't be much older than me. Well, some I guess. I wanted to ask him why, where he was going, but it was none of my business. I sure didn't plan on doing this for that long. I just want to see California and maybe start a new life there if I like it. I tried to explain that to Geri. She thinks I should have stayed and given some foster family a chance. But I think she'd be doing the same thing I am if both her parents were dead. Much as I miss Geri, I had to split. I don't know how many days like this I can handle, though.

The train gave three big blasts, then came the strain of the couplings tugging at each other. The train started moving again. Liberty Two jumped up, pack in hand. He looked down at me.

"Comin'?"

The pain in my ankle wasn't about to let me run. All my cuts stung even more now. Jumping the freight didn't seem possible for me.

I shook my head. "Naw. Hurts to move too much. Besides, it's the wrong way for me."

He nodded, took a couple of rubber bands from his pocket and used them to wrap the bottom of his pant legs around his ankles. He saw me looking puzzled. "Keeps your pants from getting caught in the wheels. Well, nice meetin' ya'. Get someone down the line to show you how to use the Internet. Good luck." He slipped on his backpack and headed for the train, looking both ways to see if any railroaders were checking for riders.

I slumped back against a tree. With Liberty Two gone, it felt lonesome, and I didn't want that feeling. But he was the first person I'd really talked to since leaving home. He sure knew a lot about hoboing. It would have been good for me to have traveled with him a while, learned a few tricks of the trains.

I closed my eyes, wondering what I was going to do now, when someone tapped my shoulder. I jumped about ten miles above the atmosphere.

"Sorry," Liberty Two said. "Didn't mean to scare ya'."

Well, he did. I admit it and couldn't have hidden the fact, either.

"You didn't catch the train." I tried to sound calmer than I was. "Miss it?"

"No. Got to thinkin' about you here alone, banged up and all. Didn't seem right to leave you since you don't know the ropes yet. Guess I'm tryin' to be a good member of H.O.B.O. Anyway, I've got no place special to go. But, if you don't want me around, I can split. Not tryin' to butt in or anything with your own plans."

"You're not buttin' in. No way. Be glad for the company. I've got no real plans except, like I told you, to get to California." I admit I was happy to see him. I dropped my suspicions and figured he was lonely, too, and didn't see me as any threat to him.

He tossed his pack on the ground and sat in front of me. "I don't know about you, but my backbone's gnawing at my belly button I'm so hungry. Got anything to eat?"

"Not much." I dug through my pack, glad I could offer him something.

I pulled out a gooey bag, wet from the smashed peach and banana I'd brought along. The last half of a ham sandwich was soaked in juices. "Crap! Look at that!"

Liberty Two gave a little laugh. "You're gonna have to learn to pack better."

"Sorry," I told him, now hungrier than ever.

"Can you walk at all?" he asked. "Might be best if ya' tried. Those knee scrapes will make it harder to walk later if you don't stretch 'em out now."

"Sure." I tried not to show it hurt when I stood up. "But where we going?"

He grinned. "Get breakfast."

"The bulls took all my money," I told him.

Liberty Two sniggered. "Shoot, it's a rare day I've got any. But there's not a day goes by I don't eat anyway."

I had no idea what he had in mind, but I got the feeling I was about to get another lesson on being a hobo. I grabbed my stuff and limped in pain along after him. Heading through the clump of trees and away from the tracks, he seemed to know where he was going. I didn't know how, because I didn't think he'd ever been here before either.

We weaved through the trees without saying anything. I started getting used to my aches and pains by the time the grove began thinning out. It got hotter as the shade of the trees disappeared. Pretty soon my sweat revived the stink of my shirt. A bunch of flies fell in love with me and whizzed in circles around my face. Somehow ants had caught wind of my bloody scrapes and made their way up my legs. I had to keep stopping, pull up my pants legs and flick them off. I felt like screaming out my misery, but held it in wondering if Liberty Two knew what he was doing.

Did I know what I was doing?

A black, crack-paved road appeared.

Liberty Two stopped at the edge and looked both ways.

"Go right," he said and started walking.

I don't know why he picked that direction and no longer cared. I dragged myself along, but all I really wanted to do was stretch out in a cool tub of water, forget why I was here, why I had no home.

But my stomach growled for attention, and that was enough to keep me goin' along. That and curiosity on where and how we'd get food with no money between us. It was a lesson I was going to need from here on in.

# CHAPTER 4

I HAVE TO GIVE IT to Liberty Two. He guessed right. About fifteen minutes later, we saw a sign, "Danville, population 2,300." Another five minutes and there was the edge of town. As we rounded a bend, I thought I was stepping into a set of an old Western movie. A weathered, falling-down structure sat on the left with a peeling Coca-Cola sign on one wall with no windows. Across the street was a one-story clapboard building once painted white, but now as yellow as an old dog's tooth. The wooden sidewalks stood off the ground a foot or so. Danville had been here a long time, I guessed.

Things changed pretty quickly once we stepped up on the wooden sidewalk, which lasted just long enough to take us past a few more run-down buildings. Then, like "Open Sesame," a new town appeared. Well, not really new, but newer anyway. Brick and concrete buildings, storefront windows with nothing much in them, an overhead sign announcing Danville's three-story hotel, which looked closed, Jake's Repair with feet sticking out from under an old truck, one gasoline pump in front, Lucy's Luncheonette, parking meters with a few beat-up trucks in front of them. It was mid-morning, too hot now, and no one on the streets.

"Kinda weird, huh? I mean, no one out at this time of morning?" I said more than asked. I felt like I'd stepped from a Western into an old episode of the "Twilight Zone."

Liberty Two stopped and nodded. "Looks like the town's been hard hit. Lotta people outta work all over."

"Think we should head back to the tracks?" That's what I wanted to do. The town just didn't feel welcoming.

"Naw. Nothin' to eat there. We'll find somethin' up ahead." He pointed and started walking toward Lucy's Luncheonette. I limped along, thinking they'd never let us in the place. We smelled and looked like bums. I said so to Liberty Two.

"Hey, we're not bums. We're hobos. There's a difference," he said.

I started to ask what the difference was when he left the sidewalk and went between two buildings, me behind him. We ended up in some kind of alleyway behind Lucy's place. Liberty Two found what he was looking for. He turned and looked at me with a grin that said I told you so, then went right to it.

A beat-up, once blue dumpster marked up with graffiti.

I watched while he lifted the lid, hung halfway in, and started picking through the garbage. I'd seen homeless people sifting through garbage cans and city trash bins at home, but I never thought I'd be doing it. The smell was anything but appetizing. I don't know what I expected when I left home, but it wasn't this. I guess I had imaged hobo jungle camps like I'd read about in a history book. Places along the tracks where poor freight riders could drop in, share what they had, get fed what they called Mulligan stew or whatever was available, tell stories about their travels. Would I ever find that?

"Come on. Help me look."

I was hungry. Neither of us had money. So, if I wanted to eat, well . . .

I took a deep breath and dug in.

"You take that side. Move things carefully," he told me. "Sometimes you find stuff that's still pretty clean. Restaurants and gas stations are good places to look. They have to rotate their food supplies. One time I found two cartons of chicken nuggets left over from the day before that they had to toss."

The thought of eating anything found in the mess of flattened boxes, plastic bags, dirty napkins covered in lipstick and mustard, coffee grounds and floor sweepings made me wonder how hungry I really was. When Liberty Two held up a slice of burnt toast with a bite out of it, he offered me a piece. I shook my head. He shrugged and shoved it in his mouth.

I held up a well-gnawed chicken bone, smiled, and threw it back in.

"Hey! What you two think you're doin' there?"

The raspy voice made us both jump and turn. A short, round woman with unnatural flaming red hair stood holding a garbage can ready for the bin.

Neither one of us spoke. We just stood there, caught, embarrassed. At least, I was.

The woman shook her head. "My, god, you two look like somethin' the trash can spit out."

She set the garbage can down. Her head kept shaking back and forth like she'd just discovered the eighth and ninth wonders of the world.

"Did you find enough to eat in there?" she asked, hands on hips.

Liberty Two spoke right up, not embarrassed or ashamed. "No, ma'am. Just a piece of toast so far." He gave her his crooked smile.

"Move aside," she ordered.

We did, and she picked up the trashcan and emptied it in the garbage dump. "Maybe you'll find better pickins in that pile," she said and turned to go back in the door she'd come out. But before she went in, she stopped. "Hell's bells." She turned to us again. "Wait here and stay outta there." She nodded at the dumpster then she went in.

"She's gonna call the cops. Let's split." I started limping down the alleyway. My appetite deserted me.

"Naw, man. The lady's cool. She's gettin' us some food," Liberty Two said, all-knowing.

I wasn't too sure about that. She didn't seem one bit friendly to me. I wanted to beat it. The last thing I needed was a run-in with the law and them finding out about me running away.

The door popped open and out she came, back first. When she turned around, I saw a plate in each hand. She held them out to us. Liberty Two grabbed his immediately. I hesitated long enough for her to say, "Well, you want it or not?"

Scrambled eggs and two pieces of toast and a strip of bacon. I took it and mumbled a puny thanks.

"Here." She pulled two forks from her apron pocket. "You two smell too bad to let you in. When you're through, set the plates by the step. There's a water spigot over there." She tossed her head in its direction. "Water's good to drink. Now don't let me catch you around here again, or I'll sic the law on ya'." She started back in.

"Thanks, Lucy," Liberty Two said with his mouth full.

She hesitated, mumbled something, then went in, the door slamming behind here. I felt bad I didn't thank her better.

My hunger came back in time to enjoy the first food I'd had in a long time. Soon nothing was left on our plates, which we rinsed off and stacked by the door. I placed my fork on top, but Liberty Two put his in his pack. I didn't say anything, and he just shrugged his shoulders. "They got plenty more."

We drank water from the faucet and splashed some on our faces. I couldn't believe our luck. Well, my luck in running into Liberty Two, anyway.

We walked away down the alley, then cut back between buildings and came out at the street again. My ankle felt swollen, but I did my best to ignore it.

"Let's see if this burgh has a library," Liberty Two said.

I followed along like a puppy after its master.

We walked a couple of blocks, passing a few people, not many. Most didn't give us a second look, like they were used to seeing scruffy teenagers drifting around town. Then Liberty Two saw something.

"Perfect," he said. "Come on."

It was a public restroom at the edge of a small, rundown park with brown grass and scrubby bushes that hadn't been watered or cut in a long time. We went in the men's side and took care of much needed business.

Without speaking, we both understood this was a good place to clean up. The sink was rusty and there was no hot water. But it served its purpose.

"You first," Liberty Two said, pulling off his shirt. That's when I saw the tattoo at the base of his neck. A hawk or an eagle with its wings spread.

I didn't want to stare, so I stripped off my shirt and splashed water over my face and chest. Liberty Two handed me a tin cup from his pack. I filled it and then dumped the water on me a little at a time, trying to rub off the sweat and dirt. I splattered water under my arms and did the best I could. There weren't any paper towels, just one of those hot air blowing machines which didn't make drying off easy. It surprised me it worked.

I noticed Liberty Two was taking off his shoes and pants, so I did, too. I filled the cup a few more times and tried to clean my lower body and wipe around my scrapes without a washcloth. With no towel, I had to use the tail of my gross smelling shirt.

While Liberty Two washed up, I put on my clean T-shirt, but decided to save my other clean pair of jeans. My knees stung worse than before and rubbed against my jeans. My elbow didn't look too hot either. Before I had a chance to ask, Liberty Two must have seen me looking and told me to get the first-aid kit from his pack. I dug through his stuff and found it, but not before I saw a six-inch switchblade knife.

His knife was bigger than the one the guy stole from me. But it reminded me of the one I had on the train when those two guys tried to get Geri and me a couple of years ago. I can't help but wonder if they would have used it on me if Geri hadn't pushed me off the train before she jumped. She keeps saying I saved her, but the truth is, she saved me, even if I did get pretty banged up. At least she came out okay.

Thinking about her gave me a sudden pang of homesick. Well, the memories of a past home, anyway. But as soon as I put that antiseptic stuff on my elbow, I sprang back to the present. How can something that stings so bad be good for you?

Anyway, we cleaned up best we could with what we had. Liberty Two advised me to roll my dirty clothes and tie them on the outside of my pack until we had a chance to wash them.

We left the men's room a bit wet on the floor and went back to our search for a library. A ghost town would have more people moving about than this one did. Maybe because it was getting too hot, or maybe that sign lied about how many people lived here. Felt kind of creepy. But the thought of sitting in an air-conditioned library sounded pretty good to me even if I didn't feel like walking all over town looking for it, if it existed.

When we passed a public phone, I suggested we check the phone book for a library address. But someone had swiped it. We stood there trying to figure out which direction to take when a black and white pulled up to the curb along with a short blast from its siren to get our attention.

"Would you boys mind getting in the car?" a cop in all his blue uniform glory asked.

It was more a demand than a question.

# CHAPTER 5

"**S**OMETHIN' WRONG, officer?" Liberty Two asked.

I admired his coolness next to my instant fear. The last thing I wanted to do was get in that police car. I did not want to be sent back to Allonia.

"Depends. Get in."

I opened the back door and we got in, holding our packs on our laps. The black leather-like seats held the heat and I felt caged in with that metal screen between the front and back. I freak out in closed in places.

The cop got out of the car and leaned into the open back window. "You boys aren't from around here. What's your story?"

"Lookin' for the library," Liberty Two answered.

"Library? What would you two want with a library? Care to show me your library cards?" He looked pleased, like he'd just caught two of the most wanted.

Liberty Two laughed, more at ease than I was. "No, sir. Not being from here, we don't have a library card, but we need to get some information there."

"Got any identification? What's your names?" His eyes went back and forth from Liberty Two to me. My clean shirt was fast getting a good dose of nervous sweat.

I couldn't believe Liberty Two. The lies tumbled out of him tied with a silk ribbon.

"My name's Rick Glass, and my friend here's Jim Thorpe."

Jim Thorpe? My name was Jim Thorpe?

He lied on. "See, we're on our way to Rockford, just outside Chicago? Gonna' visit my aunt there. We stupidly left our packs unattended at the train station in Springfield while we played these video games and while we weren't lookin' somebody stole our tickets and money."

"Un-huh." The cop looked at our packs, then back at Liberty Two. I couldn't tell if he was buying it. "Mind opening up those packs?" He opened the door, meaning he wanted us to get out, so we did.

We opened our packs. Then he asked each of us to hand him our packs. He poked through them, then handed them back. I waited for him to say something about Liberty Two's switchblade, but I guess he missed it. He needed lessons from the railroad bulls.

"Why didn't you call home and tell your parents what happened? Couldn't you call them collect?" Sweat was starting to run down the sides of his face.

Liberty Two shook his head. "No, sir. They're out of the country—traveling on vacation. That's why they sent me to my aunt's."

The policeman took off his hat and wiped his brow with his handkerchief. He turned to me. "What about your parents? They on vacation, too?"

I nodded and forced out a "Yessir." I hoped he wouldn't ask me more questions.

"So how'd you end up here?" he asked, suspicion all over his face.

Faster than I could have thought of anything, Liberty Two answered, "Hitch-hiked over. Nice lady gave us a ride. Trouble is, she had to drop us off here, just outside of town."

"Hmm. You seem bright enough to know hitch-hiking's dangerous."

"Yes, sir. It wasn't very smart of us, for sure, but we sorta' panicked and like thought maybe we could get a ride to Chicago."

"Un-huh. Thought you said your aunt lived in Rockford." The cop thought he had Liberty Two.

"Yes, sir, I did. And that's where we're headed. But at home we always talk about my 'Chicago aunt.' You know, same thing, really, Rockford's so close and all."

I hoped so. I had no idea where Rockford was.

The cop looked away and then back at us. "And the need for the library?"

Quick as a flea jump, Liberty Two came back with, "Well, see, we now know we'll never make it to Rockford hitch-hiking, so we thought maybe the library would have phone books of the Chicago area, and we could look up my aunt's phone number and call her to find out what to do. Or maybe e-mail her. Do you know if the library has computers connected to the Internet?"

Man, Liberty Two could really sling it.

Before the cop could answer, a police call crackled in over the radio. He motioned for us to get back in the car, which we did. When he answered the call, he told somebody on the other end that he'd see to it. My nerves didn't let me pay too much attention. I worried the call had something to do with us. Maybe Lucy called the cops after all.

"Okay, boys, some business I have to take care of. I'm not sure I swallow what you've been telling me, so I'll check out your story later. I'm going to drive you over to the library. And I want you to stay there until I get back, understand?" He gave us an official, stern look.

I nodded in relief, and Liberty Two, still slinging it, told him how nice it was of him to give us a lift, it being so hot and all.

When he dropped us off at the library, he sat in his patrol car and made sure we went in. I peeked through the glass door of the library and watched him wait a minute, then pull away. With the cop gone, I allowed the cool air inside to bathe me.

"Come on," Liberty Two said, "we don't have much time."

"For what?" I just wanted to enjoy the coolness.

He didn't answer. I followed him to the main desk where he asked the librarian if they had computers hooked to the Internet. She said they didn't, because their budget couldn't afford it, and that they were scheduled to close next month, Liberty Two thanked her and turned away with a frown. I don't know what he was thinking.

Then he turned back to her and asked where the closest place was where we could catch a train. Of course, she thought he meant a passenger train. But now I could see what he was getting at.

He thanked her and then we headed back to the door. No police car in sight.

"Let's split."

The outside heat hit hard as we hurried around to the side of the building and out of sight. We stood close against the brick wall in the shade. What was I doing here? Now I not only hid from the railroad bulls but from a small town cop. Things weren't moving along the way I had thought. But then, I hadn't really given my leaving too much brainwork anyway. And if it hadn't been for Liberty Two, I might have been caught on that last train. I was learning in more ways than one.

"We can't risk the roads with the cop on our butt. We gotta make it back to the tracks," Liberty Two said. "We'll follow them into the train yard in Chinoa. Somebody there will know a schedule. If not, we'll try the library there."

I nodded. Why not? I didn't have a plan.

"Don't worry. You'll get to California." He paused. "Eventually."

"No hurry, I guess." Except with all that was happening and could happen, I was beginning to wonder if I shouldn't hurry.

Like a couple of thieves, we sneaked through the town and back into the trees. Once there, we stopped to rest in the shade. My pack turned the back of my shirt into a wet sponge. And I was hungry again. I tried to fill my stomach with the memory of the eggs, toast and bacon the woman at Lucy's gave us. Didn't work.

I saw Liberty Two pull up his pant leg and slip his knife from the top of his sock and put it back in his pack. I had to admire him.

"You were pretty cool with that cop," I told him.

He grunted and stretched out flat, hands under his head.

"I couldn't think as fast as you did. Stolen money and tickets. Hitch-hiking. Parents on vacation. An aunt in Rockford, wherever that is. Sheez. How'd you come up with all that?"

He shrugged. "I did have an aunt in Rockford. Maybe she's still there, I don't know. Figured if that fuzz wanted to check out my story, I'd give him her name and hope she was still there."

"Think he'll come looking for us?"

"Naw. Why should he? He didn't want to have to deal with us anyway. He probably knew it was all a lie, but he was doing his duty. Probably relieved to find us gone."

"You told him my name was Jim Thorpe. You said I needed a new name. I like that. Maybe I'll use it from now on." I said the name aloud a couple of times to get used to it.

"Better not."

"Why?"

"You never heard of Jim Thorpe? He was a great athlete, man. Best in track, baseball, football, you name it. Won two Olympic Gold medals back in 1912. But 'cause he was an Indian and better than most, the jealous powers-that-be made up some reason to take his medals away. Gave 'em back—after he died." Liberty Two snorted his disapproval.

"How come you know all this?"

"That's the trouble with hangin' around libraries. Sometimes you read a book or two. Anyway, pick another name. If that cop does look into us, you don't want that name followin' you."

"Listen. Speaking of names, you mind if I call you LT or just Liberty?" I asked. It sounded easier.

"No problem." He sat back up. "Ready?"

I wasn't, but I nodded and hated the feeling of my sticky shirt when I slipped on my backpack and said so.

"Listen, be glad for the heat. Comes winter and you're still out doin' this, well, you'll be wishin' for this heat."

I hoped I wasn't still doing this by winter.

We took off down the tracks. My ankle was a lot better. I tried to tell myself not to let the heat get to me. Pretend I'm in the Foreign Legion in the desert. Be tough. Think about something else, like that time Geri and me—I—walked up the river, balancing on the rails, pretending we were high wire artists. If one of us fell off, we'd yell. "Splat, you're dead!" But we always had a comeback. "Saved by the high diver's water tank." Or something stupid like that.

I hoped nothing as bad as what happened then would happen this time.

I should have known better.

# CHAPTER 6

I T LOOKED LIKE the tracks went on forever. Down the line, the heat made them look like long, slithering snakes. Every step rubbed my sore knee. I knew it had started bleeding again because it was sticking to my pants. I had to take my backpack off until my arms got tired carrying it. Then I'd slip it back on, usually over one shoulder or the other.

I had a fierce thirst, and started telling myself off for not preparing more before I'd left. Geri and I had been smart enough to borrow Randy's canteen before our hikes up the river. But this time I'd blown it. Too big a hurry to get far from those welfare people trying to stick me in some strange family. Now I was paying for it.

Liberty Two didn't seem to mind the heat. He walked at a brisk pace, sometimes even jumping from one track to the other. At one point he started marching like he was in the army and sang out in an old, mixed-up cadence call:

"You had a good home when you left.
"You're right!
"Your mama was there when you left.
"You're right.
"Count off;
"Left, right.
"Count off;
"Left, right
"Count off, left, right;
"Left, right."

Sometimes when he'd sing left, he'd land on this right foot, but I didn't say anything. I couldn't have cared less.

If he was thirsty he didn't show it. I couldn't help wondering what the last four years of his life had been like. He didn't seem to be unhappy, and he knew his way around. He must like riding the rails, because that's all he seemed to do. A real modern-day hobo, and a member of a Hobo organization, if it really existed. Who knew, with LT.

I slogged along asking myself why I couldn't be more like LT. Enjoy the view, I told myself. Except not much to see that interested me. Thick wheat fields standing straight up on one side of the tracks; on the other side, a farmer raising thick, brown dust with a tractor off in the distance. Utility poles spaced every few yards, a few birds resting on the wires. Pretty quiet except for the occasional buzzing cicada and snapping bugs. No shade. Just heat and flies and gnats and endless tracks.

After what seemed like days, the wheat field ended at a dirt road inside a wire fence. Not far off stood a bunch of big, leafy sycamore trees. Liberty Two left the tracks and headed for the slight cool of the shade. My step picked up a bit as I followed him in. We both picked a tree and made it our home.

I looked up through the still leaves and noticed how covered with dust they were. Like me, they needed a good dousing. Not likely, with no clouds in sight.

We sat in silence, both happy to be out of the sun. After a little flat-on-my-back rest, I sat up to check my knee. I had to pull the sticky jean material away from my knee before I could pull up my pant leg. It didn't look as bad as it felt.

LT tossed his first-aid kit at me, and I went through the cleaning routine again. I thanked him and gave it back. I wanted a drink of water so bad I would have taken on another skinned knee in trade. But I wasn't going to say anything to Liberty Two. I was beginning to think he was part camel.

"Think I know what to call you," he said.

"Yeah? What?"

"Tripper."

"Why?"

He pointed to my knee. "Seems to fit."

I wasn't sure I wanted to be known as Tripper. Made me sound too clumsy.

Before I had a chance to say anything, LT asked, "You smell somethin'?" He sniffed the air.

I sniffed. "Like what?" I didn't smell anything except humidity.

"Stay here," he said. He went off deeper into the trees like he was stalking a wild animal or something. I lost sight of him. He must have trusted me, because he left his pack with me.

Before long, he came back, not so quiet this time.

"Come on, Tripper. Got a surprise for ya'." He grabbed his pack and waved at me to follow him.

I followed a short distance down a slope to a clearing in the trees. LT put a finger up to his lips and pointed. Then I smelled it. Something cooking.

A group of men sat on wooden crates and logs talking softly among themselves. An old black man with the whitest hair and beard I had ever seen stirred a big pot made from an old cut-down oil drum that sat over a fire. A rope had been tied between two trees and some blankets and underwear were tossed over it. A small stream ran behind the man stirring the pot.

We stayed hidden behind trees and listened.

One of the men was saying, "Yeah, I miss old Steam Train Maury. Man knew everything needed to be known about rail-roadin'. I mean everything. How many times was he voted King of the Hobos, Fry Pan?"

The one stirring answered. "Oh, four, maybe more. Can't recollect."

"Five," another said.

"Shoot, Tank Car, how'd you know? You're too young to re-member Steam Train," Fry Pan said as he examined whatever was in the pot.

Tank Car, younger looking than the others, seemed offended. He stuck out his scraggly bearded chin and scratched it. "Hey, maybe I didn't know him personal like you, but I bet I know more about the man than you do."

"And just how could that be, pray tell?" Fry Pan asked. "I traveled some miles with the ol 'bo."

"Yeah, well, I read his book, I did." Tank Car nodded for emphasis.

"His book?" Fry Pan stopped stirring and looked at Tank Car.

"Didn't know he wrote a book, did ya'?" Tank Car asked, pleased.

"Well, now, I don't believe ol' Steam Train ever wrote no book. The man never sat still long enough to write more than a letter that I recall."

"Well, he did. Wrote it with some fella, don't remember his name. But he did write it, and I did read it, and it won't be hard to prove the next time you go to a library. You do know what a library is, don'tcha, Fry Pan?"

Some of the men started to laugh at the two, and I guess LT figured it was a good time to announce ourselves. He waved for me to follow him as he headed for the group of men. "Hi, there, gentlemen. Mind if a couple a 'bos join in?"

I waited a few steps back to see what was going to happen.

A couple of the men jumped up, not too happy looking. No one said anything. They just eyed Liberty Two. Then one of the men yelled at LT. "Come here!" Right about then, another one spotted me and his gruff voice ordered, "You, too!"

We moved closer, and the men surrounded us. A varied looking bunch, some ageless, some old, but tough looking. None of them kept their hands in their pockets. It didn't give me a good feeling.

"Road kids," one of the men said. "More damn road kids."

"Spies," the one called Fry Pan said.

They all nodded and mumbled in agreement.

"What you think we oughta do with them, Hopper Bill?" the one called Tank Car asked.

Hopper Bill threw the cigarette he was smoking on the ground and crushed it with his thick-soled shoe. He wore those railroad-style overalls over a white dress shirt. A tie, stuck inside the overall bib, was pulled loose from his collar. He pushed his Dodger baseball cap back a bit on his head before he spoke. "What do you boys want?" Curly red hair fought to get out from beneath his hat. His close trimmed beard left a face darkened from the sun. I guessed he was the head honcho.

Never shy, Liberty Two spoke up. "Wouldn't mind a little somethin' to eat, sir. Smells mighty good."

"What you boys doin' here, anyway? Out for some fun, are you? Think trampin' around and bummin' off people is fun and games?" Hopper Bill looked LT over real good, then me.

Liberty Two dropped his smile. "We ain't tramps and we ain't bums. We're train riders, and just as good as you."

"That so?" Hopper Bill raised a thick eyebrow.

"Yeah, that's so. This here's Tripper and my name's Liberty Two. I'm a member of H.O.B.O."

The men were quiet for a moment then they all snorted and laughed.

Hopper Bill never cracked a smile and put his face in LT's. "What makes you think we're riders? How do you know we aren't a gang of thieves? How do you know we won't rob you of your packs there, and your clothes, and then do a little drum beating on you? Rat-ta-ta-ta." He pretended he was beating on a drum.

Then he turned to me. "How do you know we won't make you our slaves? Maybe turn you into dopers, if you aren't already, and make you run delivery errands for us?" He opened his eyes real wide. "Chances are good nobody knows where you runaways are and wouldn't even miss you if they did, now would they?"

He pulled his cap over his forehead and rubbed his big hands together looking at Liberty Two. "H—O—B—O, hah. Maybe we're members of the Freight Train Riders Association, ever think of that?"

That thing called panic rushed through me from top to bottom. Was it possible these guys were no better than the ones who stole my money? I had nothing to buy my way out with this time.

Liberty Two let his pack drop and stood his ground, fists at the ready. "Well, if that's what you are, then get started with your dirty work. I ain't afraid of you—any of you. I can take care of myself, and I'll whip anybody who tries anything funny with me."

Some of the men sniggered.

Hopper Bill moved closer to LT. "Snotty talk like that can get you killed, boy."

I wanted to run away before my heart exploded with fear. But I couldn't let Liberty Two take the brunt of this mess. He'd been too good to me to just cut out on him. I dropped my pack and stood there waiting for the worst day of my life to happen.

# CHAPTER 7

"**I** AIN'T TRYIN' to be snotty. I just came from Iowa a few days ago and joined H.O.B.O. and thought maybe you men might be members and willin' to share some grub," Liberty Two told them.

Hopper Bill looked over at me expecting me to say something. "Well? You ready to fight, too, are you?"

I don't know how I managed, so dry-mouthed and all, but fear can cause strange things to happen. I spoke up sounding braver than I was. "We don't want any trouble, sir. If you want, we'll move on." And I couldn't have meant it more.

Hopper Bill scratched his chin. "You know how many punks like you two . . ."

"We ain't punks," Liberty Two interrupted. "We don't steal, we don't do drugs, and we don't beg. We're hobos and proud of it."

Hopper Bill scoffed. "Proud hobos! Do you think saying you're a member of this, what did you call it," he paused between each letter, "H—O—B—O makes you so special?"

"I—we—ain't special, but we ain't punk kids. Shoot, you don't even know what H.O.B.O. is. I been railin' for four years and can take care of myself," LT told him.

Fry Pan spoke up. "Well, your mouth's railin' on, that's for sure. You're lucky you're still alive, you smart-assed kid. This is a dangerous life. Go home to your mamas." He looked at me. "You ain't sayin' much, bub."

LT spoke up. "He's new at this, but I'm teachin' him."

"Yeah? Like what?" Hopper Bill asked. He tapped a finger at his forehead. "Takes knowledge and skill to be a good railroader."

"I know enough," Liberty Two said. "I know how to move around a freight yard without getting' run over. I know enough not to crawl under no boxcar even if it's not movin'. I've been taught by some of the best on the rails on safe ways to jump on and off a rolling train car. I can judge the speed of a train and know you don't jump on if you can't count at least three lug nuts on a wheel. I know it's a dangerous life, but I've also met 'bos who'd offer a fella somethin' to eat and not rag on him about being young and—" he looked at Fry Pan and gave the word back, "smart-assed."

The men looked around at each other with knowing looks. I thought for sure that last remark would get the men to beating on us. But instead, they burst out laughing. LT and I gave each other confused looks.

Hopper Bill cocked his head and grinned. "Well, 'bos," he said to the men, but looking at us, "I think maybe we've got some possible railroaders here."

"I'd say," Fry Pan said, grinning. "Smart-assed ones, anyway."

"Just testing you, boys," Hopper Bill said, smiling. "Can't be too careful these days, though. We run into a lot of no-good young punks hanging around, think they're hot stuff doin' drugs and drinkin' and stinkin' up the place wherever they go. Stealing stuff off the trains—off us, even. Cops chasin' after them, then us. We don't want to get involved in any of that. What say, fellas? Shall we let these two join us for dinner?"

Each man, I counted six of them, nodded, giving approval.

"Okay, then. You two grab a pan over there on that box. Let me serve you up some of the best Mulligan stew you ever did eat." Fry Pan pointed to a wooden crate. I noticed there were some beat up pots and cups stacked inside the crate.

We didn't have to be told twice, although I admit I was still a little afraid of the unknown and these men. But I borrowed some of Liberty Two's confidence, and took a tin plate. Fry Pan gave us each a big helping and then told the rest of the men to come and get it.

I didn't know what I was eating, but it was good. No one said much while we ate. We all thanked Fry Pan and told him how good it tasted. We even got seconds.

After we ate, LT apologized about not having anything to throw into the stew, so he offered up our services and we went down to the little stream and washed all the assorted tin plates, plastic dishes and the big cooking tub.

I got a better look at the campsite once I was full and calmed down. It was a small clearing, surrounded by old sycamore and maple trees. The ground was pretty packed down and looked like the place had been used a lot. An old wooden orange crate stood on end, containing a bunch of books and magazines. Some big cardboard boxes folded flat were stacked up off to the side. I wondered if these men lived here all the time.

After clean-up, we all sat around the cook fire embers even though the evening was still warm. The daylight started to fade through the trees.

"So, what were we discussin' before we were so rudely interrupted?" Fry Pan asked the group.

"Steam Train Maury," Tank Car said. "I offered he'd been elected King of the Hobos five times and you wasn't havin' none of it."

"Just seems strange that I traveled some with the man, like I said, and never knew him to write a book," Fry Pan said.

"Well, it was after he'd done railroadin'. Got sick and couldn't do trains no more. But he got famous and gave talks to schools, jails, Salvation Army places, and like that. Why, he even went to Congress one time speakin' up for the hobos." Tank Car shook his head like he couldn't believe it himself. "Say, there's a picture a him with Dolly Parton in the book."

"Oh, get out!" Hopper Bill said. "Why would Dolly Parton want her picture taken with Steam Train?"

"Told ya'. He got famous. He was an educated, dignified, clean, stand-up gentleman who loved to ride trains. People wanted to meet him. He made sure people knew the difference between a hobo and a tramp," Tank Car said.

"Well, I sure wanna read that book before I die." Fry Pan sounded like he didn't believe a word Tank Car was saying.

"You should be westbound already, old man," the one they called Whistle Stop teased. His shaved head made him look like a bowling ball with a stubby nose.

"Don't get sassy with me, young fella. I still gotta lot of eastbound in me."

I didn't get what they were talking about, but Liberty Two whispered to me that in hobo talk westbound meant dead or dying.

The men laughed, and it got quiet for a time. Hopper Bill broke the silence. "So, judgin' by what you call yourself, I guess you know old Liberty, do you?" he asked LT.

Liberty Two nodded. "Yes, sir. Do you know him?"

"Met him once or twice. Heard about that H.O.B.O. thing you mentioned. Thought about joinin' up." He pushed his cap back and stretched his arms behind his head.

"Don'tcha think it's a good idea?" LT asked.

Hopper Bill sighed. "Oh, sure, but it'll never work. Us old-timers are slowly fadin' out of the picture. Camps like this are growing few and far between. Too many homeless and young punks ridin' these days. They know nothing about real hobo life or what it means to be a hobo . . . present company not counted, of course."

A few laughs around, then a man named Harmony started playing "I've Been Workin' on the Railroad" on his harmonica. Almost one by one, we started singing along, some of us off key, but that was okay. When we finished, someone asked Sailor to play his Jew's harp. Harmony joined in and pretty soon we were clapping and encouraging them both to play songs, like "Box Car Blues," "3:10 to Yuma," and "Big Freight Train Carry Me Home." Hopper Bill and Tank Car jumped up and started dancing a jig. I was surprised at how many songs were about railroads.

The sun went down, and even though it was still warm, more wood was added to the fire so we could see. I forgot my fears and found myself feeling at ease among these men. This was what I thought hobo life would be like.

With the music and dancing, a part of me felt better about what I was doing. But another part of me wouldn't let go of that homesicky, lump-in-the-throat feeling I get a lot in the evening for some reason. Didn't make sense, though, getting homesick for a home I didn't have any more and never would again.

So I clapped along a little louder to shut down that part of me. This was, after all, the life I left home for.

We were having a great time when the distant sound of hound dogs interrupted our music. Their howling and whining grew louder, and then they were in our camp. Flashlight beams came bouncing through the trees right after the dogs. Voices started shouting before we saw who owned them.

"Hands on your heads! All of you! Stay still or the dogs will do more than lick your face!"

# CHAPTER 8

ALL AROUND US stood men with shotguns, rifles and pistols. One of the dogs started sniffing at my sore knee. That made one of the men suspicious of me, I guess, because he put his light in my face and demanded my name.

I almost said it, but caught myself and said, "Tripper."

"Tripper? What kind a name is that? That your alias?" He kept the light in my face. Over his shoulder, he called out, "Hey, boys, I think I got one of 'em!"

More lights in my face. The dogs kept sniffing my knee like it was a bone they wanted to gnaw.

"Here's another one," someone said behind me.

They pushed LT so he stood next to me. I guessed they were looking for young guys since they ignored the others. Then I had the sinking feeling they were looking for me. Or maybe that cop back in Danville reported us.

"Where's the other one?" we were asked, hands still on our heads.

"What other one?" Liberty Two asked.

"Don't get smart, sonny. We know you stole those boxes of DVDs off the freight car you were ridin'. Where's your third partner?" He wore a tan, short-sleeve uniform and a big star-shaped sheriff's badge on his chest and his cap. He was for real. Some of his men started looking around, even going through our packs.

Too shook up and unprepared for getting hassled twice in one day, I couldn't talk. But LT had no trouble. "We don't know anything about any stolen DVDs, sir."

"Yeah, and I got two heads," one of the deputies said.

Another one spoke up. "No sign of the stolen goods here, Sheriff."

"Then why'd the dogs lead us here?" The sheriff looked agitated. "Speak up, boys. Your missing third take off with the loot, did he?"

"Sir," LT said, "there's only the two of us. We don't know anything about any stolen stuff."

I kept being amazed at how polite and calm LT talked.

"Excuse me, officer," Hopper Bill spoke up. "May I say something?"

Real gruff, he said, "What? You know anything about those DVDs?"

"No, sir, I don't," Hopper Bill said. "But I can tell you right out these boys didn't steal anything. None of us did. We've been here a couple of days now, mindin' our own business. I can tell you, these boys aren't the ones you must be looking for."

The one who said he had two heads broke in. "But that's not what my dogs say, sheriff." You could tell it was important he didn't want his dogs to be wrong.

The sheriff seemed annoyed by the dogs around my leg. "What the hell you got under your pants, boy?"

I took my hands off my head and started to pull up my pant leg when someone grabbed my arm.

"Hold on there!" the sheriff said.

Two guns were aimed at my face. Twice in one day I'd had to face guns.

"You got a weapon under there?" the sheriff asked.

"No, sir." My voice quivered, and I wished I could sound like LT.

"Slow, now. Real slow, pull up that pant leg," he ordered.

I did as told, pulling away the material stuck to my knee. That brought some fresh blood to the surface.

The dog owner said, "Probably got that running away with the goods, didn't ya'?"

I didn't want to address this dork as "sir," but I knew by now that politeness was necessary in situations like this.

"No, sir," I managed. "I haven't stolen anything. I don't know anything about any stolen DVDs." I felt proud I said so much in my defense.

"You sure there's no sign of them around here?" the sheriff asked his group.

They assured him there was nothing.

"Well, boys, I'm gonna have to take you in 'til we get things sorted out." The sheriff reached for handcuffs in a black pouch on his belt.

"Sheriff, I can vouch for these boys' innocence," Hopper Bill said.

That surprised me. He didn't even know us. For all he knew, we could have stolen the stuff and had an accomplice somewhere getting rid of the goods.

"Yeah, right. I should take the word of a bum like you. Maybe you're in on this, too. Maybe you're like that slimy character in that Dickens book that teaches kids to steal for him. What's the name?" he asked in general, snapping his fingers.

"That'd be Fagan, from *Oliver Twist*."

The sheriff threw a light at the voice. Tank Car, hands on his head, gave a shy grin and shrugged his shoulders.

"Yeah," the sheriff said, surprised as I was, "that one."

Hopper Bill said, "I'm sorry you see me in a bad light, officer. I may be down on my luck and homeless for the time being, but I'm not a thief, and I have tried to encourage my boys to go back home."

"Your boys?" the sheriff asked with a tone of doubt.

"Times are hard for some of us, Sheriff. I had to leave home and look for a job somewhere, anywhere. These foolish boys showed up here, against my wishes, thinking they could find jobs with me, help out and all. We were just saying before you showed up, how they didn't give their mama a second thought, running off like they did. They're young and not too good at thinking things through. You know how kids can be. Got kids of your own, Sheriff?"

And I thought LT could stretch the truth. But talk about smooth. Hopper Bill almost had me convinced. I just didn't know why he was saying all this.

"Yeah, I got three—wait a minute here. Just wait a minute. You're telling me that these are *your* boys?" The sheriff pushed his hat back, looked down at his feet, then pushed his hat forward and scratched the back of his neck. He blinded LT and me with his light trying to see some family resemblance, I guess.

The man holding the dog leashes spoke up. "But what about my dogs, Sheriff? They're never wrong. They're on to somethin' here, I know it."

"Shut up, Fergus. I don't know what's goin' on here."

Tank Car, hands still on his head, spoke up. "Like Hopper says, these boys aren't thieves. None of us are. The dogs just made a mistake this time."

Fergus noticed Liberty Two was scratching one of the dogs behind its ears. "Get away from my dogs! Put your hands back on your head!"

"You and your damn dogs. Get 'em away from here, Fergus," the sheriff ordered. He put his gun in its holster and waved to his men to put up their guns. "Okay, here's the way it is. None of the stolen goods seem to be around here, so I won't take anyone in, though I could on suspicion."

He looked at Hopper Bill. "You claim these boys are yours. They're bound to get in trouble runnin' loose. You can see that. So, tomorrow I want you to take those boys home. I'll be back here to check on you, and I don't want to find you here or anywhere near. Understand?"

"No problem, sheriff," Hopper Bill said. "Plannin' on doing that anyway."

The sheriff pulled out a pad from his back pocket. "Let's have a name," he told Hopper Bill.

"Bill Hopper."

The sheriff wrote it down. "Where you from?"

"Chicago."

He wrote that down. "Street?"

Hopper Bill cocked his head. "Well, that's a hard one. See, we got evicted, no money for rent, so the family's staying at a Sally."

"A Sally? What's that?"

"Oh, sorry. Salvation Army house."

The sheriff shook his head and let out a big sigh. "Okay. So give me the boys' names."

"That one there is Christopher and that one," he pointed at me, "that's John." He nodded and smiled. "Named 'em after my brothers." He gave me a wink. Earlier I was Jim Thorpe, then Tripper, now I was John Hopper. I had plenty of aliases.

The sheriff wrote everything down, shut his little book and put it back in his pocket. "I'm putting all this in my report, and I'm going to check out your story." He flashed his light around, taking everything in. "Like I said, I'll be back here at noon tomorrow, and you'd better be on your way to Chicago with your boys."

"We'll be gone, Sheriff." Hopper Bill said. Then he added, "I hope you find those three boys you're looking for. Young punks like that need a good stretch in juvy hall."

The sheriff looked at LT and me, still not sure. "Okay, then. Fergus, let them dogs loose again and try to get them to find three boys this time."

Fergus let the dogs loose. They sniffed around in circles. Then Fergus yelled, "Come on, you stupid four-legged mudfarts. Do what I trained you to do."

But the dogs just kept sniffing in circles, then lay down.

The sheriff shook his head. "Face it, Fergus, they've lost the trail. Give it up."

"They've never done this before. I don't understand. There's somethin' fishy goin' on here."

The sheriff shook his head. "Let's go, boys," he called out to his men. Then he looked back at us. "I heard about this camp. Afraid I'm gonna have to find out whose property you're on. I don't want to make trouble, but it may be I have to close this place down. Like I said, tomorrow."

None of us spoke as the sheriff and his men faded back into the trees. We watched the beams of the flashlights grow dim and then gone.

Then, sputters, sniggers.

"Hopper Bill, you could make a snake think it's a dog," Fry Pan said.

"Shh!" Hopper Bill whispered. "They might be listening in there, lookin' to catch us up."

We all went silent and stared into the dark trees.

# CHAPTER 9

AFTER A TIME, Hopper Bill said, "I guess it's safe now. Just talk natural."

We all relaxed and some of us gathered around the dim fire again. Fry Pan threw some wood on for some light. Nobody said anything for a bit. Then Harmony started playing a song I didn't recognize on his harmonica. A couple of the men said goodnight and went off to their blankets.

Tank Car looked at Hopper Bill and chuckled. "Bill Hopper. That's a good one."

Hopper Bill smiled and nodded.

Of course that wasn't his name. I should have known he wouldn't give his real name. Nobody here used his real name. But why did he lie for Liberty Two and me? I wanted to ask but wasn't sure I should.

Liberty Two did, though, straight on. "Thanks. Really appreciate what ya' did," LT said. "But why'd you lie for us?"

"Well, now, I hope you're not calling me a liar." He stretched out and leaned up against a crate.

LT said, "Calling us your sons ain't exactly a truth." He gave a nervous little laugh.

He pushed his cap, covering his eyes. "Ah, but I never said you were my sons. Never once used that word. I called you 'my boys' and as long as you're in this camp, you are my boys."

"That's right," Sailor said. "He never called you his sons. Sheriff just thought that's what he meant. And he did try to tell you boys when you first stumbled in here to go back to your mamas. That's no lie."

"You told him our names were Christopher and John. That's a lie, ain't it?" LT asked.

I didn't like him trying to make Hopper Bill out a liar. He'd just saved our necks, and I was willing to let things alone. Even if he had stretched the truth a little. Now LT acted like he thought something suspicious was going on.

"Boy," Hopper Bill said with exasperation, "I thought you knew about hoboin'. If you did you'd know you never use your real name. Someone tags you and that's it. I tagged you Christopher and him," he pointed at me, "John. Those happen to be my brothers' names. So now you're Liberty Two Chris and your friend there is Tripper John, though we ought to call him Bloody Knees John."

"Yessir," Fry Pan chimed in, "Them hound dogs sure loved sniffin' your knees. Ha! And how about the look on the face of that one called Fergus!"

Harmony imitated Fergus. "But, sheriff, my dogs ain't never been wrong."

I laughed along with the rest of them.

But LT wouldn't give up. "Bet you lied about being from Chicago," he said to Hopper Bill.

I got peeved at LT. Why was he pushing it so hard?

Hopper Bill sat up and gave LT a hard look. "You lose, kid. Now, let me give you another little lesson about this life you've picked to live. When somebody helps you out, you say thanks. You don't ask for their life story. It's none of your business. You've said thanks. Now, I suggest you leave it be." Then he added, "And quit saying 'ain't.'"

LT nodded and looked down at some design he was drawing in the dirt with the toe of his shoe. "Sorry." He paused. "See, I know about that Freight Train Riders Association you mentioned. A bad bunch. Just needed to be sure about you. Truth is, not knowin' us and all, I can't figure out why you done it. Especially since now on account of us you're gonna have to leave the camp tomorrow before the sheriff gets back."

"Shoot, I'm not worried about that sheriff. If he does come lookin' you two will be long gone." Hopper Bill took off his cap and scratched his head. It surprised me that he had a little bald spot.

"What about you?" Liberty Two asked Hopper Bill. "Sheriff'll be lookin' for you, too."

Hopper Bill slipped his hat on the back of his head. "Not your problem. I just want you two gone first light, understood? Get yourselves over to Chinoa and catch anything that'll get you far from here."

I surprised myself when I spoke up. "Yes, sir. First thing." Then a meek, "Thanks for helping us out. We didn't steal anything," came out of my mouth.

Hopper Bill yawned and pulled his cap over his face. "Never thought you did, son."

Most of the men started bedding down for the night. I noticed they used the folded cardboard under their blankets. Liberty Two pulled his blanket from his pack and motioned for me to join him away from the fire pit. We moved into the shadows near the trees. I spread out my bag next to LT.

"Why'd you try to get Hopper Bill all riled up?" I whispered.

"Can't figure out why he stuck his neck out for us, that's all. He don't know us. Maybe he thinks we did steal those DVDs. Maybe he thinks he'll horn in on us and expect a cut of the loot. I don't know. But the joke's on him, 'cause we didn't steal any . . ." Liberty Two stopped when we heard someone's movements nearby. A form looked down on us.

"Couldn't help hearing what you said, boy, but you can rest easy." With a few creaks and groans, a form squatted down close to us. "Age sure does take away the spring in your bones."

The moonlight lit up his cotton white hair and whiskers, his face lost in the dark.

"Mind if I join you'all?" Fry Pan asked. "I'd like to tell you a little story."

"It's your camp," LT said. "We're the guests."

Fry Pan didn't say anything for a moment. "That's true. You're the guests. Uninvited guests," he emphasized. "And, boy, you got an attitude that needs a little mannerin'."

"I don't mean no disrespect to you or any one. It's just that I've been on the road a long time now. Seen a lot. Much of it no good, manners be hanged. I've been taken advantage of before, big time, and I don't mean to let it happen again."

"So you think Hopper Bill or one of us is out to do you harm?" Fry Pan asked.

"What he did tonight? Gettin' the sheriff off our backs and all? People I've been meetin' don't do things like that for strangers unless they got a reason, especially when the law's involved."

Fry Pan leaned over in my direction. "What's your opinion, young fella? You think your partner here is right?"

"I don't know. I mean, everything happened so fast. I was so happy to see the sheriff go I never had time to think too deep on it," I answered.

"Well, think on it now," he told me.

"Well, I did wonder why Hopper Bill spoke up, but I never thought there was a bad reason for it," I admitted. "But I'm not as experienced as Liberty Two, so I don't know what to think."

"You boys like history?" Fry Pan asked.

"Not really," LT said. I had to agree. It always bored me in school.

"Here's the thing, see. I'm short on advice, but long on history," Fry Pan said. "Me and Hopper Bill, we got a history. We go way back. What I'm gonna tell you is none of your business really, but I'd like to think all history doesn't have to repeat itself."

Liberty Two and I looked in each other's direction. Even though we couldn't see the other's face very clearly, we wondered what this old man was getting at.

Fry Pan gave a rusty cough. "You boys ever hear about the orphan trains?"

We both told him no.

"Course not. Well, here's a little history lesson to put in your pocket that ain't in most history books. Back a long time ago in New York City my parents died and I had no place to go."

Like me, I thought to myself.

"I was just a little tyke and couldn't take care of myself. Relatives couldn't afford to take me in. Somehow, don't rightly recall, I was put in this Children's Aid home. It wasn't too bad once you adjusted to the lonesome way of life there. Anyway, when I got to be around ten years old, I found myself and a bunch of other kids from the home on a train headin' west."

Liberty Two interrupted. "They put you kids on a freight?"

"Naw, it weren't no freight. An old Pullman car with those scratchy seats. Anyway, they told us that we were all headed for adoption. The children's home had so many kids they couldn't afford us all. It was cheaper to ship us out west somewhere." Fry Pan stopped, remembering something, shook his head, then went on.

"Well, the adoption part didn't sound too bad. Some of us had visions of living in a nice home, with good food and step-parents, maybe a room of our own, school, stuff like that. Maybe some got that. I didn't. No, I got dropped off in Michigan with ten others. What we got was three meals a day for workin' long days in the field and the pleasure of sharin' a converted hay loft bedroom at night." Fry Pan paused again, remembering things.

"Like a work camp, was it?" Liberty Two asked, wanting him to go on.

"Felt more like being a slave."

"Did the Children's Aid place know what was going on?" I asked.

"Don't know. I'd like to think they didn't."

"So how long did you stay there?" LT asked.

"Too long. I didn't know where I was in Michigan, had no money, and didn't know where to go even if I ran away."

"How'd you get out?" I asked.

"A couple of the boys were older'n me. They always talkin' about escapin' and hoppin' a train back to New York. Then one day three of us were workin' way out in the field where the owner couldn't see us. The boys decided to make a break for it and I followed. Didn't really know what I was doin' but went along anyway. I guess I was ready for a change." Fry Pan grabbed one of his legs and started rubbing it hard. "I get the jumps in my legs sometimes. Can't even climb on a movin' train no more. My train days are in the decline."

Fry Pan quit talking and we waited. Then LT spoke up. "So what happened?"

"Got caught right off. They took us back to the farm, but the man there didn't want us any more. Said we'd be nothing but trouble. So we all ended up in a kind of juvy detention. Really a kind of jail work farm."

"Excuse me, but what's this got to do with Hopper Bill?" LT asked.

"Runnin' on, am I? Here it is then. When I got to be eighteen, they let me go. I had no money, so I took to the rails. Needed to get some place new. Well, I just kept goin' to some place new for lots of years. Trains took me all over this country until one day, I met Hopper Bill's daddy."

"His daddy?" Liberty Two and I said together.

"I told you I was long on history," Fry Pan answered.

"Yessir, saved my life, Conductor did." Fry Pan sighed the words.

"Conductor?" Liberty Two asked.

"Hopper Bill's daddy. He got that name 'cause he actually was a ticket conductor once. With the Union Pacific, I think it was. But as the way things happen, he lost his job."

The moonlight faded between some clouds and trees, so we could no longer see each other clearly. I stretched out on my bedroll, my pack plumped up under my head. It felt good. I was ready for the day to be over and, to be honest, so tired I was only half interested in Fry Pan's talking.

Liberty Two yawned and asked, "So how'd he save your life, this Conductor guy?"

"They were gonna hang me."

That caught my attention.

# CHAPTER 10

"YEAH," FRY PAN went on. "I'd caught me a boxcar just outside of Denham headed for Baton Rouge. Bein' the only black man among the group ridin' I sat off to myself. One of the men asked me where I was headin' and I answered politely as I'd learned was a good thing to do. 'Runnin' away, are ya, boy?' someone else asked. I said, no, I wasn't runnin' away, just going some place new. 'Think he's the one?' another voice asked. A couple of them moved closer to me until my back was against the wall.

"Well, let me tell ya boys, I started gettin' that fast fireball of fear that works its way up from your stomach and burns in your throat, eyes and ears. Then one of 'em said, 'Maybe there's a reward.' Another one ordered me to stand up. 'I'd say he fits the description, wouldn't you?' this other fella says. 'He's black, for sure,' another says and they laugh.

"I finally found my voice. 'I don't know what you fellas are talkin' about. I swear I ain't done nothin' wrong,' I told them. I stared into their faces looking for some one to believe me, but un-un. No, sir. You know, some days, like now, when I tell this story, I can still feel the fright and anger raging through my old bones."

Fry Pan went quiet for a moment. A dog howled off in the distance and a few bugs snapped at the air near the fire. Liberty Two and I waited, a little more awake now.

"Well, anyway," Fry Pan went on, "there was some talk among them about turning me in at the next stop. By now most of the men were positive they'd get a reward for turning me in."

"What was it they thought you'd done?" Liberty Two asked.

"Fools thought I'd done somethin' bad to some white girl. Can you beat that? Why, I'd never in my life even talked to a white girl back then."

"Well, what happened?" I had to ask.

Fry Pan cleared his throat. "Now this is where the story gets interestin'. A deep voice I hadn't heard before comes out from a dark corner behind the men, 'Leave the man be. He's not the one they're looking for.' He made his way through the group and looked me square in the eyes. A big man, he was. Red curly hair, broad shoulders, still wearin' part of his conductor's uniform. Well, I learned that later. Anyway, I look right back at his eyes so blue they shined in the dim light. At least they did that night. He asks me, "You been near Masden town the last twenty-four hours?' I tell him, no, I just got out of that work farm outside of Denham where I been for the last few years. Never been near Masden. He tells the men how if they'd think on it, they'd realized where I got on the train and that I couldn't have got on there if I'd been over in Masden. But some of those ol' boys, they taste that reward idea and try to argue until Conductor says, and I'll never forget those words, 'You leave the man alone or you got me to deal with'."

Like lightning, that old saying, "Like father, like son," flashed through my head. Conductor had stepped in and saved Fry Pan just like Hopper Bill stepped in for us tonight.

"Well, there was some grumblin' that occurred, but nobody wanted to challenge Conductor. He looked big enough and tough enough he could pick you up and throw you across the railroad yard if he'd a mind to. Besides, his uniform made him look official." Fry Pan made a little clicking noise with his tongue.

"Now, I know you boys is wonderin' why he would do that for someone he didn't know and wasn't even the same color, especially back then."

"You got that right," Liberty Two said.

I nodded, forgetting no one could see me in the dark.

"Simple. The man had goodness in him. And you saw tonight how it rubbed off on his son."

"Goodness," LT said flatly.

"Yessir, goodness. Now, in this life that's somethin' you don't see every day. No, sir, it's rare in many a man I've run across over the years. Oh, I've seen little acts of goodness. One man loanin' something to another. Sharin' food and campfires and such. But to stick your neck out there all alone when it could get chopped clean off, well, that's true goodness toward your fellow man."

"So what happened when the men in the boxcar backed down?" LT asked.

"Well, now, that's gonna be even harder to believe," Fry Pan said. "Things stayed quiet in the car for a while. Then the train started slowing down. Conductor came over to me and said, 'When I tell you to jump, jump.' Well, I thought hoo-boy, the man done turned on me and there was gonna be trouble after all. I didn't say a word, just nodded my head. Then Conductor tells me bulls gonna be checkin' the trains at the next stop and that word's gonna be out that they lookin' for somebody to hang for what happened to that girl."

"Did you believe him?" I asked.

"When he said 'jump,' I jumped."

"Well, you're still tellin' your story, so I guess he was on the level," LT said.

Fry Pan chuckled. "You got that right. The man saved my life, for sure."

"So you must have met up with Conductor again. Otherwise, you'd never know about Hopper Bill bein' his son," I said.

Fry Pan's leg twitched and he started rubbing it. "Feels like ants in my bones."

"Yeah," Liberty Two asked, "how'd you meet up with him again?"

Fry Pan muttered something about his leg, then went on. "Here's the thing of it. Conductor, he jumped off the train with me. Turns out his wife and son—that'd be Hopper Bill—lived nearby. That's why he was on that train. And just my good luck, too."

"Why's that?" Liberty Two asked.

"That man . . ." he paused, shaking his head. "That man invited me to come along with him to his home. Can you beat that? He didn't know me from Adam, yet he invited me, a black man, to his home."

"So I guess Hopper Bill was here, huh? That's how you met him?" LT asked.

"Oh, yeah. Guess he was 'bout the age of you boys."

"So, what happened?" I asked. "That was a long time ago. Is Conductor still around? I mean, how come Hopper Bill's ridin' the rails? How come you two are together now?"

Fry Pan took a deep breath and let out a sigh. "Well, now, that's a sad story."

# CHAPTER 11

WE WAITED, saying nothing. I began to think Fry Pan wasn't going to tell us any more. He'd already told us a bunch, and I thought 'bos weren't supposed to tell personal stuff that wasn't any one else's business. So I kept quiet.

But Liberty Two couldn't.

"Come on, Fry Pan, what happened? You can't stop now. How come you and Hopper Bill are travelin' together after all these years?"

Fry Pan scratched his white-whiskered chin. "Guess I been gabbin' a lot, huh?" He looked into the dark toward the fading fire. "Guess it won't hurt to say."

But he didn't say anything.

"Come on," LT coaxed. "You started the story. Finish it."

Fry Pan let out another one of his soft sighs. "It's like this. Old Conductor was on his way home because his wife was sick. He'd been searchin' around for another job after getting laid off. When he got word about his wife, he bee-lined it home." He paused. "But it was too late. His wife done died that very day. That very day. Can you beat that?" He shook his head. "Hopper, 'course that's not his real name, was sittin' by her bedside cryin', not knowin' what to do, half happy to see his dad, half mad 'cause he'd been gone so long."

I related to that in my own way.

"Anyway," Fry Pan went on, "I kinda' felt in the way and said so, but Conductor, he said he'd appreciate it if I'd stick around and keep an eye on Hopper while he sorted out the funeral stuff and the like. So I did. A day or two led to a week or two, then a month. Hopper and me, well, we hit it off pretty good. Anyway, the Conductor, he tried to get a job in town, but there was nothin'.

Well, he took me by surprise and asked me to watch out for young Hopper while he went off lookin' for a job. Said he'd send for the boy when he got settled. After he'd been so good to me, how could I say no? So, he left us most of the little money he had with him and took off."

Fry Pan stopped and started cursing his leg again. He rubbed it pretty hard, then went on. "Anyway, Hopper took his troubles like a man. He didn't give me no use to be sorry I'd said yes." Fry Pan shook his head. "Shoot, he sure loves to correct my English."

Like Randall did, I thought to myself. He was always correcting Geri and me.

"He'd kid me about it a lot, but it never did no good as you can tell. He finally gave up. Old habits die hard, they say." Fry Pan stopped, like he'd lost his train of thought.

"Let me guess," Liberty Two said. "Conductor never came back."

"Well, now, that's true enough. But not because he didn't want to. No, sir, he truly meant to. The thing is, old Conductor, he got himself jammed between two cars when they were coupling up. Got dragged to death when the train started movin'."

Neither LT nor I seemed to know what to say. All three of us stayed quiet until Liberty Two spoke up. "Did you tag Hopper Bill with that name?"

Fry Pan laughed. "Oh, yeah. First time we hit the rails. We were ridin' on a flatcar when we saw some bulls makin' their way down the line of cars lookin' for riders. The only thing we could do was move back down the train. But there were no good cars for hidin'. Now the last thing you want to do is get in an open hopper car when it's carryin' a cargo, especially coal. But that's all we had. So we hid ourselves under the coal in that dirty old hopper. The wind whipped the coal dust all around us. Terrible time tryin' to breathe. Tryin' not to cough until the bulls passed by. Terrible."

Fry Pan paused, then continued. "Never did that again, for sure. Anyway, when we finally got out of that filthy situation, I looked at Chris, I mean Hopper, and broke out laughin'. His face was as black as mine with the whites around those blue eyes stickin' out like headlights. His cap was covered with soot except for the bill. Don't know why, but that durn bill stayed clean as soap powder. So I tagged him Hopper Bill."

"Cool story," LT said.

I agreed.

"So there you have it, boys. You got nothin' to worry about with Hopper Bill. You're lucky he understands what it's like to be without folks and on the move."

"Yeah, and he's lucky to have you," I said.

Fry Pan nodded. "Maybe so. Works both ways, I guess. Still, I'll always owe my life to Conductor."

"I'm just sorry he has to leave on account of us," I said.

"Ah, don't worry 'bout that. Hopper's got itchy feet. We'd a been movin' on soon anyway."

I couldn't tell what LT was thinking, but knowing all that made me feel a lot better.

Fry Pan got up and started back toward the fire embers. "Best get some rest, boys. Tomorrow's got your future waitin'."

LT and I said goodnight to each other and stretched out on our blankets. I looked up through the trees and noticed the stars for the first time. They looked just like they did at home when the night was clear. I couldn't name one star over another, but I got used to some of the shapes they made. I kept thinking I should take the time to learn some constellations, or at least be able to identify the North Star. Geri knew some of them and she'd point them out. "There's such-and-such a star," she'd say. She'd get excited when she found the Big Dipper. I missed her.

I stared up at the stars. The sky looked so big, and I felt as small as one of those tiny lights. I probably would have cried, the way I felt right then, but I had promised myself I never would again.

I lay awake thinking about Fry Pan's remark about my future waiting. I hoped I was as tough as I knew I'd have to be to survive it.

# CHAPTER 12

*I* TRIPPED AND FELL. The man with the club beat me on the sole of my foot. I couldn't figure out how he could hold me down, flash the light on my face, and beat me at the same time. He kept calling me names. I wanted to get up, but I couldn't move. I just let him beat on my shoe. I tried to say, "Leave me alone," but no words would come out.

"Come on, Tripper. Wake up. We gotta get outta here before noon." Liberty Two was shaking my foot.

I sat up on my elbows and looked around. It took me a minute to realize where I was.

"You okay?" LT asked, shoving his gear in his pack.

"Yeah, bad dream."

Looking over where the fire had been last night, I saw some of the men sitting around drinking what I guessed to be coffee. The line that held the blankets and clothes the day before was down. I tried to spot Hopper Bill and Fry Pan but I didn't see them.

"Tank Car said we could have some bread and coffee if we wanted some. You want any?" LT asked. "I do."

"Sure." That's when it hit me that we had to leave. Who knows where we'd be tonight, or where our next meal would come from. I stuffed my bedroll in my backpack and LT and I walked over to the rest of the men.

We exchanged some quiet good mornings. I looked around for Fry Pan and Hopper Bill, but didn't see them.

Tank Car handed each of us a couple of pieces of bread and motioned us to help ourselves to some coffee in a pot sitting on a gas camp stove. "Old Fry Pan and Hopper said to tell you fellas good luck on your journey," he said. "They took off first light."

"Where they goin'?" I asked. It was none of my business, but I actually felt a kind of sadness that they were gone, a loss of something I couldn't explain.

"Didn't say," Tank Car answered. "Reckon we all be clearin' out right soon."

As a group, we didn't say much. When we finished our breakfast, LT asked me, "Well, you ready?"

I nodded and then we said our thank-yous and good byes. As we left, Harmony played the tune for "Anchors Aweigh" on his harmonica. We turned, and he gave us a big grin and a thumbs up.

I hoped the next group of railroaders would be as friendly as this group had been.

Liberty Two and I left the wooded area and made our way back to the tracks. It was early, but already getting warmer. As we walked along the tracks toward Chinoa, I asked LT about the Freight Train Riders Association. "Are they like the H.O.B.O.?"

"For sure—NOT!" he said with emphasis. "Those guys are worse than the bulls. They'd cut your throat for your worn-out toothbrush."

"Ever run into any of them?" I asked, starting to sweat already. I wished I had washed off a little in that stream before we left.

"Nope, and don't ever want to." LT hopped up on a rail and balanced himself with outstretched arms. He could stay up way longer than I could. But then, he'd had lots of practice.

When we neared the town, I realized I might be traveling alone today. LT was headed for Chicago, and I was headed for California. I got that sinking feeling again. Last night, hanging out around the fire, singing, listening to Fry Pan and all, well, it was like I wanted things to be. It was more like what I'd read about hobo camps. I started to worry about being alone. LT had shown me a lot, but not enough for me to feel I knew what I was doing. Just the opposite. And what if I ran across those Freight Train Rider guys?

"So, you gonna take off for Chicago today?" I had to know.

Liberty Two didn't answer and didn't look back. He kept his

balance on the rail for quite awhile. When he finally slipped off, he said, "Probably. Maybe. Depends."

I caught up with him. "Depends on what?"

He looked at me and grinned. "Depends on which way the first train's going."

I nodded, not saying anything. Then it came to me that I had no deadline for getting to California. Maybe I could travel with LT for awhile if he'd let me. He could be my school until I felt smart enough to graduate.

We walked for maybe half an hour before we saw the outskirts of Chinoa. As we got closer, the tracks split. LT pointed to the right and we followed those tracks into town. We didn't see any trains. LT told me to keep my eyes open for railroad workers, but I didn't see anybody. A small workers' shack sat between the two sets of tracks, but it looked locked up. A few empty auto racks used for transporting cars and two tankers sat on a side line.

LT motioned for me to follow him behind one of the tanker cars. "Not much action in the yard here, so it looks like there won't be anything comin' through for awhile. Anyway, we need to get some food and water before we go catchin' any train. Let's hide our packs here and go into town and see what we can scrounge up."

The bread and coffee had long worn off, so the idea appealed to me. I hoped the town had another Lucy who might help us out, but I knew better. The thought of digging in a dumpster put me off. Still, if that's all there is, what are you going to do? I figured I was about to find out.

The mid-morning heat was starting to build along with my hunger. After hiding our packs in a stack of railroad ties, we walked toward some taller buildings like we knew where we were going. LT figured our pickings would be better in the business section of town. As usual, I followed along, glad to be with LT.

When we got to what we thought was the center of town, we walked along the shady side of the street. We passed a bank, a feed store, two or three boarded up places, a fabric store, a plumber's shop and a hardware store. No restaurants or coffee shops. Not much on the other side of the street either, just a gas station and more shops. My hunger grew more fierce, making me feel mighty low.

We gave up on the main street and walked a block over. On the corner we saw a parking lot, and then the sign: Chinoa Supermarket. We headed for it.

"Thar she blows!" LT called out. "Ready your harpoons for action, men." He rubbed his hands together.

Since we had no money, I didn't see why he was so happy to sight a grocery store. Then I realized the whales LT sighted looked a lot like two blue dumpsters.

No one seemed to mind the two of us digging through the garbage. Most people passing paid no attention. Some smiled. Some shook their heads. Still, I was embarrassed, even though no one knew me.

It turned out one of the dumpsters was what LT called a bonanza. We actually "harpooned" some stuff worth eating, enough that I went in the store and asked for a plastic bag. I was given one with no questions asked. We filled it with some unsquished oranges, a loaf of bread with just a little greenish mold on the end pieces, some broken carrots, a couple of onions, three potatoes, a halfway dented can of baked beans, and some smashed boxes still half-full of Corn Flakes. We had to wipe a lot of goop off some things, but they looked okay once we did. Standards change when you're hungry.

Grinning between bites of carrots, we headed back to the railroad yard. On the way, we filled our water bottles from a garden hose coiled up by the side of someone's house. No one came out to yell at us.

Our packs were still where we left them. We sat in the shade of the stacked railroad ties. LT took his knife from his pack and stabbed away at the can of beans until it opened. Tossing away the moldy bread pieces, we ate our fill of bean sandwiches and sucked the juice from the oranges for dessert. We split up the rest of our findings and shoved them in our packs. LT had this idea we'd make a stew for dinner with the veggies.

I started to ask him how and where he thought that would happen when we heard voices. LT put his finger to his lips. Peeking over the rail ties, we saw three men opening up the workmen's shack. We slumped down so they wouldn't see us, but we could hear them.

Then we heard something we didn't want to hear.

I looked at LT. His face mirrored my worry.

# CHAPTER 13

"**A**RE THEY local boys?" one of the workmen asked.

"Don't know for sure."

I tensed when I recognized the voice from last night.

"What do they look like, Sheriff?"

"Never got a good description. Three teenagers, thin, average height. One with long hair," the Sheriff answered. "Thought we had them last night. Two of 'em, anyway. Still not sure if I got fed a line or not."

"And they stole what?" another asked.

"Several cases of DVDs. Those kids probably don't know they pulled off a grand theft, so it's big time jail when we catch 'em."

"We'll keep an eye out," one of the workmen said.

"Yeah. I'd appreciate it. Last night, I ordered some bums to get outta town by noon today. Father and two sons, or so they said. They could be involved in the theft, even though I couldn't prove it. Sent a deputy out to their camp to make sure they left. I'm gonna hang around when the 12:10 for Kansas comes through. Chances are, they'll try to catch it. Is it runnin' on time?"

"Supposed to be. Hope so. Too hot to hang out here waitin'," a voice said. "Well, good luck, Sheriff."

I looked at LT. He was smiling. I didn't see anything to smile about.

He leaned over and whispered in my ear. "This is good news, not bad. Now we know what time a train's comin' and where it's goin'. Instead of catchin' it here, we'll grab it out of town aways."

That made some sense. And it sounded like LT was going to catch the train even if it was headed away from Chicago. That made me feel better.

LT peeked over the stacked ties. Then he whispered, "We gotta get on the other side of those tank cars so they can't see us. I'll go first. Then you. Try not to make any noise. Don't run. If they see you runnin' they'll suspect something. Be cool. Be casual. They're lookin' for three people, not one. Once we're on the other side of those tankers, we can head out of town and wait for the train a ways up the tracks."

I nodded an okay.

"Don't trip." He grinned. I didn't grin back.

LT peeked around the railroad ties and waited for the men to get busy and look the other way. He crouched, keeping his eyes on the men, then stood up and, like he said to do, casually went toward the tank cars. Then he was gone.

I followed his lead, doing exactly what he did, except one of the men looked my way as I stood up. He looked at me, not saying anything. My insides froze, but I managed a smile and waved at him, then turned and walked on. I wanted to run and didn't dare look back, wondering if they were coming after me. But no one called to me, so I kept walking until I got to the tanker.

"Nice goin', Tripper." LT gave me a friendly punch on the shoulder. "For a minute there, I thought you might blow it. You're learnin'."

Sweat started pouring out of me. I'd made it. And LT even gave me a compliment. But it wasn't safe to stay where we were, now that one of the men had spotted me.

We hurried along behind the tanker cars and then headed out away from the tracks to make it look like we were going into town. We meandered around past some houses and buildings and made our way to the tracks outside of town.

"Which way's the train comin' from?" I wondered aloud.

LT shrugged. "Don't make much difference. We'll take it either way."

"Yeah, but what if it takes us back through town again?"

He didn't say anything. No need to. I knew he was thinking the same thing I was. The sheriff would have the railroad people searching the train for those thieves. If they caught us, he would know we weren't Hopper Bill's kids. Then we'd probably get drilled again about the stolen goods. They'd want our real names. They'd find out I was a runaway and maybe send me back to Allonia or put me in juvenile hall someplace. I don't know what they'd do with Liberty Two. I could only hope from where we were that the train would be coming from town, not heading to it.

It was almost noon, as we figured it, and too hot to stand in the open. There was a small clump of trees and brush off a bit from the tracks. We found a little shade and sat waiting for the train.

"You ever jump a moving train?" LT asked.

I thought about the time Geri and I hopped the train going up the river road. Geri almost lost a foot. "Yeah, once," I answered. The first two trains I caught when I left Allonia weren't moving.

"A word of advice," LT said. "If the train's coming in to town, it'll be slowing down, which is good for grabbin' hold. If it's comin' out of town, it will be pickin' up speed, so we have to be quick."

"Right," I said, starting to worry. I remembered what LT said about needing to see three wheel lugs to jump on safely.

He pulled out two rubber bands and used them to clamp the bottom of his jeans. "These are all I've got. You got anything you can use?"

I shook my head.

"Well, stick the bottom of your pants into your socks the best you can. You don't want your pants getting caught on anything."

I did, realizing how dirty the bottoms of my pants and my socks were. Mom would never have let me out of the house this dirty. Homesickness tugged at me, but I fought it off.

"Another thing," LT said. "We don't know what kind of cars this train will be pullin'. We may not be able to get on the same car. If we're lucky, we'll find an open boxcar or flatcar. If so, throw your pack on and then jump for the ladder. Don't try to get on with your pack on your back."

"What if there aren't any boxcars or flatcars?" I asked, getting more worried.

"Makes it tough. Grab whatever ladder you can reach and hang on for the ride. Climb to the top of the car and find a spot to lay low. You may have to move from one car to another. But whatever you do, don't let your feet get caught in a coupling between two cars. Stay high."

I remembered what Fry Pan had said about Conductor and what had happened to him.

I guess the worry showed on my face.

"Hey, don't worry. You'll get the hang of it. If it's a long train, we'll have plenty to choose from, and it won't be movin' too fast."

"What if it is movin' fast? What if it isn't even going to stop in Chinoa?"

"Then we'll wait for the next train, okay?"

I nodded, feeling a little better.

The sun, high now, didn't give us much shade. Too hot to talk, we didn't say much. Mostly, we swatted at bugs. My clothes stuck to me, and flies and gnats did their best to annoy me. In school, I'd seen documentary movies about places like India where some natives didn't seem to mind flies crawling all over their faces. Miserable, I felt caught between not wanting the train to come and wanting it to so I could get away from the pests.

Just as I thought I couldn't take it any more, LT stood up and said, "Listen."

Two blasts from the train's horn assured us. I stood up and tried to guess where the train would be coming from. Two more blasts.

"From Chinoa?" I asked LT, hoping I'd heard right.

LT smiled. "*Adios*, Mr. Sheriff. Hope you catch the bad guys."

I smiled, too, and sighed with relief.

We grabbed our packs and moved near the tracks. I looked back down the rails toward town and watched as the diesel engine's bright, twirling light seemed to be looking for us. With each blast of its horn, the mass of iron and steel grew larger and louder. As it moved ever closer, what I saw no longer resembled a train, but some kind of mythic monster from a fantasy story come to swoop me away.

To where, I had no idea.

# CHAPTER 14

LIBERTY Two motioned for me to step back from the tracks as he did. The rumbling train pulled by three engines wobbled by us, the long line of mixed cars straining to keep up. LT waved at the engineers, but no one waved back. They seemed to sense what we were up to. But they didn't look at us long. When they turned their attention to what lay ahead of them, LT turned his attention to the railroad cars coming our way. Then he saw one he liked.

"Now!" LT yelled as he ran along side the train.

I ran, too, and watched LT throw his pack on a flatcar and jump on the small, low metal ladder. Fast, he was up and safe, yelling something I couldn't hear over the noise of the clacking train wheels.

Too late to catch LT's flatcar, I ran along side the train as it picked up speed. It seemed to be going a hundred miles an hour. The noise of the metal wheels on the tracks ground through my body. I thought I wasn't going to make it, but then there I was, running beside a graffiti-covered boxcar with an open door. I threw my backpack inside and grabbed at the highest metal rung I could reach at the end of the car. In truth, I don't know how I made it. But I pulled myself up and held on like a baby monkey to its mother.

I looked forward and saw LT wave from the flatcar. Not wanting to let go, I gave a little wrist wave back. I wondered how long I was going to have to ride hanging on to a ladder. I could feel the train pick up more speed as the wind pushed into my face and played with my hair. I was afraid to move, worried my feet might slip off the metal rung.

Soon the muscles in my legs started to cramp. I don't know how long I rode like that, but it was long enough to make me think I was seeing things. Maybe it was the wind and dust in my eyes. But I thought I saw a woman's face look out the open boxcar door.

I blinked a few times and stared at the open door. Then a head peeked out the door and back in again.

Someone was inside.

Then the head stuck out a little farther. The wind blew her long, dark hair over her face. She had to pull it back so she could see me. She got a good look at me, then disappeared.

My leg muscles felt like marshmallows and I worried they might give out on me. My arms were going numb from holding on so tight. It occurred to me that I could easily lose control of my muscles and fall off the train. Whoever was in the boxcar had my pack now, and I wondered if I'd ever get it back.

I looked toward the front of the train for LT, but I couldn't see him. My mind saw him stretched out comfortably on the flatcar and it bugged me.

Then the head stuck out of the boxcar door again. This time her hair was tied back and she stared at me. I stared back. Then she motioned for me to come to her. I thought she was nuts. How was I supposed to do that?

She yelled something, but I couldn't hear her over the track noise. Then she pointed to something along the bottom of the car. I couldn't figure out what she meant until I noticed a thin metal ledge about five inches wide along the bottom of the car.

I figured she *was* crazy. Especially if she expected me to walk along that small ledge back to the door.

But then I realized the train could go a long way with me riding like I was. I couldn't hold on forever. Maybe I was the crazy one.

I looked over the side of the boxcar wondering if there was any other way to make it to the door. I could try climbing up the ladder to the top, but that wouldn't get me inside. Then I noticed another five-inch ridge along the car about shoulder height.

That's what all her pointing and yelling was about. She wanted me to hug the side of the boxcar while holding on to the higher ledge and inching my way along the lower one.

I looked at my feet and then at the ledge. No way they would fit on the bottom ledge. I'd have to be Spiderman. I looked forward at her. She was nodding and motioning me forward. Could I do it?

I knew I could never make it to the next stop riding like I was. So I gave myself a pep talk. You wanted to be a hobo, a rail rider. You always thought you could take care of yourself. You've taken dangerous chances before. Remember what you and Geri went through? What have you got to lose? Try it.

So I did.

Slowly, I stuck one foot out to the ledge and pushed the inside of my foot up against the side of the car as closely as I could. I pressed hard, because half my foot hung over the edge. Holding on to the ladder with my right hand, I stretched my left arm out and clamped my fingers on the upper ledge. I waited like that for a minute until I felt secure. Then I lifted my right leg off the ladder and quickly placed my foot on the ledge, turning it so the inside of that foot touched the side. Letting go of the ladder was the hardest part. But I did, and grabbed at the upper ledge with my right hand. And there I was, plastered belly against the side of the boxcar, hoping I'd done the right thing.

The wind wanted to whip me off the train. Afraid to move against it, I stayed glued to the side of the boxcar. But my fingers started cramping up, because I couldn't get a real grip on the ledge. I had to move or fall off. So inch by inch, I started creeping toward the open door. Never lifting a foot, and hugging the side, I slid one foot along the ledge for a bit, then the other. One hand fingered its way, then the other. One foot, then the other. One hand, then the other.

It seemed like hours before I reached the door. When I got there, a strong hand reached out toward me. I grabbed it with my left hand, swung my left foot off the ledge and inside the boxcar. The hand pulled and yanked the rest of me in.

"I knew you could do it," the woman said.

My voice was still outside the boxcar, so I just smiled at her in relief. I couldn't tell how old she was. Maybe my mom's age—was. She had some gray in her hair. No makeup. Some wrinkles around her dark eyes. She wore a sleeveless flowered dress, kind of dirty I noticed later. The idea of a woman hobo threw me off for the moment.

We both stood there, trying to keep our balance with the swaying of the train.

"You gotta time things a little better," she said. "When your pack came flyin' in here, I thought someone would be right behind. Then nobody showed up. So I looked out and saw you almost missed the train." She folded her arms over her chest and gave me the once over.

My voice caught up with me. "Thanks for your help."

"New at this, aren't you?' she said.

I nodded. "Yeah. Slow learner," I admitted, wondering when and if I'd ever learn enough not to be labeled "new." I looked around to see if anyone else was in the car. It was dark in the corners away from the door, but it looked as if we were alone.

She pointed. "Your pack's over here."

I noticed it was open. She'd been looking through it. I stooped next to it and started looking to see if everything was there.

"I looked through your gear," she said, "but I didn't take anything. It's all there."

It ticked me off, her going through my stuff, but I didn't say anything.

"That a picture of your mother I saw?" she sat down cross-legged on an old plaid blanket she had spread out. That's when I noticed she was barefoot. Her ankle-high boots and socks had been thrown aside.

"Yeah," I said, not looking at her. I found my water and drank about half of it. I shouldn't have, because I didn't have a clue as to when I might find more. Another reminder that I was new to all this. But my little walk along the ledge gave me a fierce thirst.

"You a runaway?" she asked.

I started to say it was none of her business, but she beat me to it.

"It's none of my business, of course. I guess after seeing the picture of your mother, well, I feel sorry for her. She must miss you. Unless she knows you . . ."

"She's dead," I said in a tone I hoped let her know I didn't want her questioning me.

"Sorry. No offense meant. Sorry for your loss," she said. She turned and stared out the open door.

I put my water away, took my pack and went over to a dark corner of the car.

I couldn't stop thinking about my mother. I didn't want to. She did the best she could after dad died in that scuba accident. It was hard for her. And me. I wasn't too easy on her the last couple of years, for sure. I should have helped make life easier for her. I should have quit school, got a job. Should have paid more attention to her instead of thinking about myself. Well, too late now.

My throat got all achy and lumpy feeling. It did no good wishing things were different.

But I wished they were.

I looked out the open door, but I couldn't tell you what was out there.

# CHAPTER 15

THE TRAIN sped along, the steady clack of the wheels dulled my mind and made me sleepy. I guess I dozed off, because I jumped when her hand touched my shoulder.

"Sorry. Didn't mean to scare you," the woman said, kneeling beside me.

I gave her an annoyed look.

"Just wondered if you were hungry. I noticed you had some raw veggies in your pack, but nothing to eat. I'm fixin' to have a cheese sandwich. You want one?"

Still angry she'd gone though my stuff, I didn't want to take anything from her. But I was pretty hungry. I just shrugged my shoulders and tried to act indifferent.

"Is that a 'yes'?" she asked, smiling. Her teeth needed a good dentist.

"If you have enough," I managed, already tasting the cheese sandwich from memory.

"Well, come on over." She stood up and walked back to her space in the car, balancing herself as the train rocked back and forth.

I got up and made my way to her spread. She sat on her blanket and pulled two wrapped sandwiches out of a khaki duffel bag. She handed me one. I waited until she opened hers before I opened mine. I didn't want to look as starved as I was. Why, I don't know. Pride? Anger? Trying to look tough, experienced maybe.

The sandwich was just white bread and a slab of cheese, but I didn't mind. Once we started chewing, she said, "Pretty dry. Sorry I can't offer you some mayo and pickles."

I shrugged, not saying anything, knowing I should say thank you.

"Look," she said between bites, "I know you're pee-ohed at me for looking through your stuff. I would be, too. But you need to understand something." She stopped, like she wasn't sure she should go on.

I looked at her and waited for her to go on.

"See, traveling alone, being a woman and all, isn't easy or very glamorous." She gave a little laugh. "That's for sure." She took another bite and chewed before going on. I went back to my sandwich.

"See this?" She pulled her hair back and I noticed that a part of her ear was missing. "And this?" She turned her head and lifted her hair. A big scar.

"Like I said, it's not easy on a woman traveling alone." She didn't say anything more until she finished her sandwich. She let me put the pieces together and watched me finish the rest of my sandwich. "When you threw that pack in here, I had no idea who would be following. I went through your stuff to make sure there were no knives, guns, or anything I was going to have to defend myself against. I was just protecting myself against stuff you can't begin to imagine."

I could see her point. It made sense. She didn't take anything. I took a really good look at her and saw her for the first time. "Thanks for the sandwich."

"You're welcome. Want an orange soda? It's not cold, but it's wet."

"Sure."

We sat on her blanket, sipping warm soda and wobbling with the roll of the train.

"My boy died," she said, breaking the silence. "Car accident. Only sixteen."

"Sorry," I told her. And I was. I knew what death took away.

She nodded. "I know you know the pain, losing your mother an all."

Neither of us said anything for a time. Then she spoke up. "None of my business, like I said, but I can't help wondering why a young boy like you, like my son, would pick this life. It's hard.

It's dangerous. It leads you nowhere except from one end of the tracks to the other."

I didn't see any harm in telling her my story. So I told her about being orphaned, them wanting to put me in a foster home, my need to get away.

She shook her head. "I'm no one to give advice. Look at me. Husband ran off after our son died. No money, no job. Lost our house. Took my first freight ride trying to get to my sister's, but once I got there, her husband didn't like me around. So I started riding around, looking for work here and there. Nothing permanent ever came up. Look at me now." She smirked. "Maybe they'll vote me Queen of the Hobos." She started crying.

I didn't know what to do or say. I turned away. With no warning, another train going the opposite way wopped by with a deafening racket as we sped by each other. Then it was gone.

"Don't end up like me, kid," the woman said.

I looked at her. She gave me a weak smile.

I didn't want to end up like her. I wanted to get to California and find a job and settle down. But I couldn't help wondering, what if things didn't go the way I planned? Not that I had any solid plan. But what if I *did* end up like her? Or Hopper Bill? Or Fry Pan? Or Liberty Two?

I'd almost forgotten about LT. He was on this train, too, just a couple of cars ahead. I told her about LT and how we met. Partly, I wanted to get her mind off her own troubles. And partly, I guess I needed to talk. It felt right to talk to her, even though LT had told me not to tell people anything personal.

"That's nice you have someone to travel with," she said. "Can you trust him?"

"Sure," I answered. But after I said it, I got to thinking. In the short time I'd known him, LT had shown me a lot. He'd been helpful. But had we been in a situation where trust was involved? How well did I really know him? I had no reason not to trust him, but I couldn't really say I knew him well.

She gave me another of her weak smiles. "Well, be careful."

I knew it was the mother in her talking. I felt sorry for her.

"Headed any place special?" I asked.

"No. I'll stay in some homeless shelter next big town until my time there runs out. They only let you stay so long. If I can't get a job, which I probably won't, I'll pick another train, do the same."

I didn't ask her how long she'd been riding trains. And I wondered why she couldn't get a job somewhere. Her English was better than mine, or any one else's I'd met so far, not counting Hopper Bill's. And she seemed nice enough. I guessed her sadness had taken over. What I really wanted to ask was how she got that scar and part of her ear cut off. Then, again, maybe I didn't.

I got up to stretch my legs and looked around the boxcar for the first time. It wasn't a bad place to ride. The open door let in light like a big bay window and gave you a great moving view. The high ceiling made the boxcar seem roomy with nothing in it. At least I was in out of the wind and sun. Poor LT was riding on a flatcar and out in the open.

After a time, the fields and trees started to thin out and scattered buildings came whizzing by. Our speed kept dropping off, and we passed a few guardrails and flashing lights with cars stopped behind them. We were pulling into a town or else just passing through one.

"This will be Springfield," the woman said behind me.

"Do we stop here?"

"Depends on whether or not the train picks up or drops off any freight cars here."

A few blasts from the train's horn surprised me. The train slowed even more. Soon we were in a big train yard, tracks going in all directions, some with freight cars lined up on them waiting to be hooked up to an engine.

I looked back at the woman. Boots on her feet, she was rolling her blanket up and stuffing it in her duffel bag.

"Getting off?" I asked, wondering if I should.

"Guess I will. I'll check out the shelter services here. See what they got to offer."

I felt a little sorry she was leaving. "Hope you find a job," I told her, meaning it.

She nodded. "We'll see. Anyway, nice to meet you. And like I said before, be careful. I hope you find what you're looking for in California." She put an arm through the duffel strap and hoisted it on her shoulder. She stood by me at the open door, peering out. The next thing I knew, she tossed her bag and jumped. I watched her run a few feet along with the train, slow down, then go back for her bag. Then she was gone.

I didn't know what to do. Stay on or jump off. Before I could make up my mind, the train's screeching brakes brought the train to a jerky, grating stop, throwing me off balance.

Then there was LT, looking up at me. "Come on," he yelled, looking up and down the track.

I grabbed my pack and jumped. My mind had been made up for me—again.

# CHAPTER 16

L T DIDN'T SAY anything as we scampered over and under the couplings of all types of parked railroad cars. If a train started to move while we were jumping a coupling, we'd be dog food. When we reached a wide-open space of empty tracks, LT motioned for me to stop. I watched as he searched for any railroad workmen or bulls. I looked behind us, wondering if I'd see the woman on the train.

"Where're we going?" I asked LT, my voice soft.

He pointed. "Across this open space to those hopper cars."

That's not what I meant. I wanted to know why we got off the train, and what he was doing besides playing hide-and-seek. Maybe the train we had been on was going farther west, maybe to California. I wasn't sure I should have gotten off.

Before I got out my real question, he said, "Come on. Run!"

I took off after him.

Halfway across, my foot snagged on a track switch and I fell on my sore knee. A billion needle pricks of pain. My pack shifted on my back and threw me off balance. When I tried to catch myself with my hands, I landed on some nasty black gravel. Some of the smaller pieces stuck in my hands when I tried to brush them off. Right then, a train horn blasted so close I froze. My head ran a movie of me stuck on the tracks with a diesel engine bearing down on me. I was about to die!

I stood up as fast as I could. An engine *was* coming my way, but not on the same tracks I was on and not very fast. Another blast from the diesel's horn set me limping off as fast as I could. I didn't know whether the engineers saw me or not. I just wanted to get away from there.

LT didn't see me fall. But when he made it safe between a couple of hopper cars, he turned and saw me pick myself up and limp run toward him.

"What happened?" he asked when I got to him.

"Tripped! What's it look like?"

He shook his head, which only made me angrier. "Is this a daily practice with you, Tripper?"

All kinds of nasty remarks came to mind at that weak moment, but I said nothing. I was angry with LT, but knew it was wrong. It was my fault I tripped and fell. Right then, nothing seemed right. Like bees trying to get out of a jar, stinging confusion buzzed around in my muddled head. What was I doing here? What *did* I want?

"You okay?" LT asked, bringing me back to the moment. "We need to get out of the train yard."

"Yeah, I'm okay," I lied, putting a lid on my jar of uncertainty. My knee was killing me and my hands felt like fire sticks. "Where're we going? You know of a train headed west?"

"Hey, unless you know more than I do, there ain't no dining car on that train we were ridin'. Before we go any farther, we need to eat. There's always a train." He kept looking around for bulls.

I didn't tell him about the sandwich the woman on the train gave me. But he was right again, and that made me angry. It made sense to get food before we went any farther.

"So, what's the plan?"

"Get outta this yard, go someplace we can cook our stuff." He gave me a look. "You still got those veggies we divided up?"

"Yeah." I gave him a look back. What did he think I did with them?

He smiled and held a thumb up. "Okay, then. Let's get outta here."

The rail yard was packed with trains lined up all over the place. We had to be careful as we made our way around them and between them. Most cars sat on the tracks waiting to be emptied or loaded, but here and there a long line of them would be moving. That's when we'd had to grab a ladder at the end of a moving car, swing around and stand on the coupling, then jump, all while the train got pulled along. On top of that, the couplings that join two cars together wobbled and made it hard to stand. If you got a foot caught in one, you could say goodbye to some body parts. The condition of my hands and knee made it even harder and more dangerous.

But we made our way through and out of the yard. We walked— well, I limped—about a half a mile along a junkyard. All kinds of metal gear and wrecked auto parts stood stacked high above the wall. There was the usual heat, no breeze. I thought of a line from a song: "Body all achin' and racked with pain." That's how I felt. Secretly, I hoped we'd find another nice camp like before, maybe even run into Hopper Bill and Fry Pan. That's when I asked myself what we were going to cook our stuff in when we did find a place. So I asked Liberty Two.

"You worry too much. We'll find somethin'," he answered.

His answer ticked me off, but he turned out to be right. When we got to the entrance to the junkyard, LT walked right up to one of the workmen and asked if they had any large restaurant-size tin cans. The man pointed, and we went over and searched through a pile of cans, most of them bent or flattened. But we found a big, restaurant-sized tomato can with only a few dents.

LT felt pretty proud of himself. When we left the junkyard, he put the can on his head and proclaimed himself "King of the Tin Cans." It gave me a laugh. For about half a minute.

We walked about another half mile and came to a freeway underpass. Near an embankment, we found a clearing mostly hidden by some tall shrubs. The freeway noise was bothersome, but it looked like a good out-of-the-way place to cook our grub.

My cheese sandwich had long worn off. I wondered if LT had eaten since we'd left the camp that morning. It was hard to believe this was the same day we'd left Chinoa. And it wasn't over.

We took the food we'd divided up from our packs and put them on a red and white bandana of LT's. He handed me his knife and said, "Why don't you cut the food into pieces that'll fit the can? I'll scrounge around for some firewood."

I took the knife and nodded. He took off and that gave me a chance to look at my knee. It hurt worse than it looked. The fall had opened up my first cut, but the fresh blood had dried and it didn't look infected. At least my jeans weren't damaged.

It hurt my hand to hold the knife, but I told myself to grin and bear it. I deserved the pain for tripping. I took out my water bottle to wash off my hands and the few veggies we'd collected. My mom always washed the veggies before cooking them. But when I looked at my bottle, I realized I'd already used up half. We needed water to cook our stuff, and I didn't know how much LT had. I wasn't about to look in his gear. So I just started cutting up the potatoes, carrots and onions into pieces that would fit in the can. I tried not to think about where we got them. I tried not to think about my mom washing and cutting vegetables for our dinner, and how many times I'd told her I hated vegetables and didn't want dinner.

Cutting the onions made my eyes water. At least, that's what I told myself.

I heard the brush surrounding our little campsite snap and crackle as Liberty Two made his way back with an arm load of small wood pieces. He looked in the can, full of cut veggies. "Okay. You got any water?"

"Not much. You?"

"Enough for makin' us one heck of a stew. I can taste it already. Get my bottle outta my pack and pour it in the can. I'll get us a little fire goin'."

I did, and it didn't take him long. Once it got started, he took a stick and made a space for the can in the middle so it was surrounded by the flames. We watched as the can turned black on the outside from the fire, red around the tip. Before long, the water started boiling. LT took a long stick and stirred the stuff in the can every once in a while.

"Got anything to eat with?" LT asked.

"No," I answered, ashamed to be unprepared once again. I didn't even have my knife any more.

He dug through his pack and handed me a fork. I recognized it as the one he had taken back at Lucy's. He pulled out a plastic spoon and held it up for me to see and said, "Be prepared, as the Boy Scouts say."

He didn't pull out any plates, so that meant we'd eat out of the can. I didn't mind. Our stew started smelling pretty good to me.

Before we had a chance to eat any of it, we heard the snapping and rustling of the shrub branches we thought were hiding us. We watched as a tall, large figure wearing an army camouflage outfit stepped through the brush inside our camp circle. He threw the large heavy pack he was wearing on the ground. One side of his large brimmed hat was pinned up. A scruffy, gray beard covered his cheeks and chin. A white eye was painted on the black patch he wore over his left eye.

Hands on his hips, he stared down at us, his one good eye holding us still like bugs pin-stuck in a display case.

# CHAPTER 17

L T AND I JUST stood there, captivated and speechless. Then the eye seemed to let us go.

"What's for dinner, troops?"

He walked between us, tall even stooped over, and looked in the can. "Looks like enough for me." He stood up, rubbing his hands together. "Nice of you to have dinner waiting for me when I get home."

LT snapped out of our stupor enough to speak up. "Home?"

"You have good ears, soldier. You heard right. Home. Here." He pointed down at the ground. "This very here." Unsmiling, he focused his one eye on LT.

I know it's not true, but it sure looked for a moment like a bright ray came shooting out of that eye. LT stepped back, almost as if he tried to get away from it.

"Where's my fork?" He held out a hand large enough to cover my head.

LT, always more together than I ever seemed to be, asked, "Who are you? This place ain't your home. We found it. Nobody's been livin' here."

"Forgive me for not introducing myself." Fast as a snake strike, that large hand hit LT on the side of the head, knocking him to the ground. The guy turned and gave me the eye. I handed him the fork in my hand, expecting to get the same as LT. But he just took the fork and turned back to LT, who was holding the side of his head.

"Have more respect for your king, lad. King MacArthur's the name. King of the Crusades. King of all the wars that ever were and will be. I'm King of Medals." He stood tall and raised the fork in the air like a weapon. "Yes, that's who I am. King to and of fighting men and women all over the world. So, you see, I demand respect and will have it—or your heads."

He looked at both of us, nodded, satisfied he'd made his point. Then King MacArthur bent down and picked up the hot can from the fire with his bare hands. He didn't even flinch. We watched in disbelief as he ate our dinner. I sure wasn't about to say anything, and LT, lesson learned, kept quiet, too. His cheek was red and starting to swell.

"Needs salt and pepper," the King said.

We didn't acknowledge his comment, so he said it again.

"Needs salt and pepper."

I didn't want him getting angry, so I told him we didn't have any.

"Did I ask you if you had any salt or pepper?" That eye seemed to want to melt me.

I shook my head, wondering what it was I should have said.

"I'm just telling you. Next time put more salt and pepper in it." Finished eating, he dropped the fork into the empty can and threw them into the fire.

LT and I watched as he untied a folding lawn chair from his big pack and opened it up. He went through his bag and pulled out a bottle of whiskey and an umbrella. He opened the multi-colored umbrella and fastened it to the chair. We could hear the chair strain when he sat down. With a dramatic flair, he unscrewed the top off the bottle and took a big swig.

"Now, it's time for you lads to present the King with his due. You!" He pointed the bottle at LT. "Bring your bag before the King so I can see what gifts you have to offer."

LT and I looked at each other, agreeing without words that the King was crazy. But after the way he smacked LT, we also knew we had to be careful. I just wanted to grab my pack and run. But I hated to think what he'd do if he caught me. I guessed LT felt the same way, but I couldn't be sure. I could never be sure what LT might do or say.

LT took his pack and stood before King MacArthur.

"Bow down before your King, you cheeky lad. On your knees."

LT hesitated, until King leaned forward and gave him that eye. He knelt down, his pack in front of him.

"That's a good lad. Now, show me your gifts," King demanded, taking another drink.

LT emptied his pack, showing King everything as he took it out.

"That's it? Clothes unfit for a King? No weapons for my armory? No jewels for my treasury? No food for my kitchen?" He took another drink. "Take this unsightly junk away. Tomorrow I expect much better of you, or it's off with your head, understand?"

LT nodded.

"Say, 'Yes, my King.' "

LT hesitated, then said, "Yes, my King." He gathered his belongings and stuffed them back in his pack.

"That's better. Next!" King ordered.

I took LT's place, bowing before being told and emptying my pack. He liked nothing of mine either, except the photograph of my mother.

He held it up and made some *mmm* sounds. "Yes, a fair maiden. She will do. I want you to bring her to me. If I like her in the flesh, she can become my queen." He put the picture in the band around his hat.

I started to tell him who she was and that she was dead. Then I thought better of it. The guy was nuts, so the truth wouldn't matter, especially at this point.

"May I have the picture," I asked, worried I'd never get it back.

"Don't be little asses. I need to make sure the woman you bring me is the same. If she doesn't look like the woman in the picture—off with your head. I've been tricked before. Never again. Oh, no, no, no."

I shoved my stuff back in my pack and said, "Yes, my King," even though he didn't order me to. I hated him for taking my only photo of mom. I didn't know how, but I had to get it back.

"Now, lads, for some entertainment. How about a song? Or a dance? A story, maybe? Come, come, don't be shy."

LT and I looked at each other. LT rolled his eyes and shook his head. "You gotta be kiddin'."

King stood up. "I don't kid."

"Well, I don't sing and dance. And I don't know any stories," LT said, leaning back out of his reach.

I half expected King to knock him another good one. But instead, King just dropped his head and sighed. Then he looked up to the sky. "Why? Why am I surrounded by disloyal idiots?"

He pointed to the ground in front of his chair, meaning sit down. We did.

"Good. Now. I don't want *you* to entertain *me*. I'm quite sure you lowly subjects couldn't if you tried. No, I'm going to entertain you. So, what shall it be?" King flipped a finger up and down on his big lips, thinking. "A story, I think. Yes. A story." He took another drink from his bottle.

King dropped into his chair. It sounded as if something cracked, but he paid no attention. He paused to take another drink.

Was this really happening? My stomach growled, reminding me it was all very real. I was hungry, an angry captive, and a bit afraid.

"No doubt you wonder about my name. Let me explain. During my first war to defend my kingdom, I learned to strike at the enemy quickly. I would scout out an enemy encampment and . . ." He slapped his empty hand on his thigh. "All over before they knew what hit them. My men said I struck like a King Cobra."

He paused, slapped his thigh again, and repeated, "All over before they knew it." His mind left us for a moment.

"What war was that?" LT dared to ask.

"The Crusades, of course, stupid boy. Afterward, King Arthur himself anointed me King of the World Beyond His. But since then I've had to fight many battles over the years. Someone was always making me fight. War, after war, after war." He stood up.

"I hate war. It does terrible things to people." He drank from his bottle, swaying slightly over his chair.

"MacArthur," he said, sitting down again.

LT and I waited for him to go on, even though he wasn't making any sense. I wasn't swift on history, but even I knew he never fought in the Crusades.

He drank some more, then began again, his deep voice fuzzy now.

"MacArthur. A good general under my command. He gave me all his medals. I still have them. Let me show you." Unsteady on his feet, he went to his pack, pulled out a cigar box and placed in front of us. "Open it."

LT held the box up so I could see and opened it. It was full of military service medals. Two I recognized right away—Purple Hearts. Others I couldn't name, but by their colors I guessed they were Silver and Bronze Star awards. At least a dozen medals in all. I noticed one of the certificates in the box was an Honorable Discharge Certificate from the army for a person named Samuel Reed. That name was on the medal certificates, too. Was that King's real name, or did he steal these?

"When MacArthur died, he gave me these to keep because I was such a brave king. I decided in his honor that I'd take his name as mine. King MacArthur." He took a long drink. "All hail King MacArthur!"

He laughed, raised the bottle high and saluted with the other arm. When he snapped his heels to attention, he lost his balance, stumbled over his folding chair, fell, and hit his head on the bottle he held. He tried to get up, moaned, then lay still.

We didn't move for a minute, making sure he was unconscious. "Let's get outta here," LT whispered.

I couldn't have agreed more. I half walked-crawled around King MacArthur and grabbed my pack. LT did the same. I started to leave when LT said, "Wait a minute."

I didn't want to wait another second, but I watched as LT started going through King's big pack. The sun was going down and I wanted to get as far away from King Fruitcake as possible. LT shoved some stuff I couldn't see from the big pack into his.

"Come on," he whispered.

But I didn't. Instead, I knelt down next to the fallen King and took my mom's picture from his hat.

LT nodded approval and started looking carefully through King's pockets. He turned to me and grinned, holding up a wad of money.

That's when King MacArthur sat up and his huge hairy hand grabbed LT's arm.

# CHAPTER 18

L T TRIED to pull away, but couldn't.

Looking at no one, King MacArthur bellowed out, "Beware, lads, everything they tell you is bassackwards. Don't ball up. Being ballsy gets you medals, but they'll use your body parts for dog food and your eyeballs for marbles. You're a plaything to them. A machine they create and use. They're insidious! Oily-tongued prevaricators! They create a war but let you and me fight and die for them. They create war with septic sticks! This King knows! War is a ball-breaker and don't let them tell you otherwise!" He started to say something else and then fell back down, letting go of LT's arm.

LT jumped up, shoved the money in his pocket and grabbed his pack.

I didn't like the idea of stealing, not even from the loony giant. But I wasn't about to argue at this point. King might become conscious again at any moment, and I didn't want to be around. I started through the brush and heard LT following.

We half-ran, half-walked along the street under the freeway, not knowing where we were going. When we were far enough away that it felt safe, we sat down on a bus-stop bench. We looked at each other and broke out laughing. I don't know about LT, but for me the laughter was a release of everything, not just my latest scary adventure.

LT shook his head. "King MacArthur, right. A real nut case."

"I think his real name is Samuel something. Reed, I think. That's what it said on discharge papers and some other certificates. If they're his, he's a veteran."

"A sicko. I don't care who he is. He needs to be locked up. He smacked me a good one and ate our dinner, man!" LT pulled out the money from his pocket and counted it. "We hit the jackpot, buddy boy. Sixty-six buckaroonies. Old King MacArthur's going to buy us dinner."

Starving, I couldn't argue with that. In a way, it did seem right. I told myself the stolen money was payback for the way we'd been treated. Still, stealing was stealing. But for sure, LT wasn't about to give it back. Hunger won out.

The sun was setting and lights were starting to pop on. We walked a few blocks and found a corner shopping area with a restaurant.

"This time, the front door," LT said.

Inside wasn't very crowded. We found a booth and didn't need to look at the menu very long. LT ordered a cheeseburger with fries, and I ordered a pepperoni pizza. We kept asking for refills on water. After that, we had ice-cream sundaes.

To have a full belly for a change felt good, so we just sat there in our thoughts. I couldn't help thinking about King or Samuel. Just like the hobos I'd met, LT included, he was homeless, too. Like me, he had nobody. Well, maybe. The war, whichever one it was, had made him a hero with medals. But it looked like he'd lost his eye and his sanity. Once a hero, now a brain-fried bum. No wonder he ranted on about war. Didn't seem right somehow. Even though he'd scared me, I felt sorry for him.

I said this to LT.

"Sorry for him? You kidding? Not me, man. Who knows if those medals are really his. He could've stolen them for all we know. He sounded more like a drug crazy looney. Hey, that reminds me, look what I found in his pack." LT rummaged through his stuff and showed me.

He held up one of those compact cooking kits with a small frying pan, a pot, a cup, and a plate. "Cool, huh?" Then he pulled out a small backpacking stove-like thing. I don't know what you call it, but it has a little can of fuel attached.

"And last, but not least . . ." He held up an all-in-one tool. I'd seen them on TV. They could be used for everything from a can opener to a screwdriver. "This little baby will be most useful."

I smiled and nodded, even said, "Cool." But it was all stolen goods, no matter where Crazy King himself got it. I guess what I was thinking showed on my face.

"Hey, don't worry 'bout it," LT said, putting it all back in his pack. "You got to take advantage of what you can when you're broke and on the road. Takin' from him ain't like really stealing."

I wasn't convinced.

"By the way, where's my knife?"

I'd forgotten all about it. "I don't have it. I guess I left it where I cut up the vegetables. Sorry."

"Don't worry 'bout it. I was going to give it to you. I got this one now." He didn't want everyone in the restaurant to see it, so he passed it under he table. I held it in my lap. An army bayonet and sheath.

"Jeeez, LT." I slipped it back to him. He grinned and put it in his pack.

"You boys want anything else?" The waitress gave us a big smile and started clearing away the dishes.

"No, thank you ma'am," LT said. He was in pretty good spirits. "Just the bill, please."

I didn't want to leave the restaurant and hit the rails again.

LT paid the bill and I noticed they were selling telephone cards at the cashier.

It just came out. "LT, how about buying one of those phone cards. I'd like to call someone."

# CHAPTER 19

LT LOOKED PUZZLED and gave me a funny look. But he pulled some money from his pocket and bought the cheapest card. "Here." He handed it to me, wanting me to tell him who I was going to call. But I didn't. I don't know, maybe he didn't really care. Maybe I just wanted him to.

We went outside where I found a pay phone. "I won't be long," I told LT.

I wished the phone had a closed booth, but it was one of those open ones. Using the card, I dialed the number I hadn't forgotten. After four rings, I almost hung up.

"Hello?"

"Geri?" I don't know why I asked. I recognized her voice.

"Who's this?"

"Me—Jay."

"Jay! Where are you? Are you okay?" She sounded excited.

"I'm in Spr . . . Yeah, sure, I'm okay." I felt nervous. Why was I calling?

"Jay, I'm so glad you called. Why'd you run off like that? You've done some stupid stuff, but this tops the list, dummy. What's with you? You coming home? Everybody's worried about you. You shouldn't have taken off like that."

"You know why. I don't want to live in any foster home with people I don't even know. I've heard about how some kids are treated. People take in kids to get money from the government."

"Not everyone, Jay. My parents know the people who'd like to take you in. So do I. They're a nice family. They'd treat you right."

I didn't say anything for a minute. I saw the home I used to live in. All the stuff Geri and I did together. I did miss her. But I wanted not to.

She seemed to read my mind and asked, "And what about me, Jay? Did you even think once about me and how I'd feel? Do you think your running away is easy for me?"

I didn't answer. She was right. I hadn't thought about her feelings. I just thought she'd understand mine.

"Jay? You still there?"

"Yeah."

"Where are you? I'm really pissed at you. What are you doing? Are you living somewhere?"

It was good to hear Geri's voice, even in anger. A touch of what used to be home.

"I'm moving around a bit. Met a cool guy I'm travelin' with. I'm doin' okay." I tried to sound convincing.

"You're catchin' out, jumpin' trains, aren't you?"

I let out a little laugh. She really knew me. "Yeah."

"Jeez, Jay. I thought all that business about wantin' to be a hobo was just big talk. Didn't what happened to us change your mind?"

I flashed back to that time when Geri pushed me off the train so those guys chasing us couldn't grab me. I spent a long time in the hospital afterward.

"Guess not. Here I am." I didn't want her questioning my leaving. After a pause, I said, "Don't worry about me, okay? I'm fine."

She yelled, "How can I help not worry about you, you stubborn moron?" Then her voice softened. "I wish you'd come back. Please come back, Jay."

I didn't say anything, couldn't. Then Geri said, "Dad took care of all your stuff for you."

"What stuff?" I had no idea what she was talking about.

"You know. Everything you left behind. Your mom's furniture, clothes, stuff. You took off after the funeral, which my folks paid for, by the way . . ."

"Oh, jeez, I didn't even think about that."

"There's a lot you didn't think about."

"Tell your folks I'm sorry. Some day I'll pay 'em back." I'd forgotten that Geri's parents had helped me arrange for the funeral. There wasn't any insurance. I didn't stop to think about the bill. I just wanted to get away before they took custody of me.

"You creep, you didn't think about anything but yourself. Cripes, you make me mad. Anyway, what do you want us to do with your stuff? Should we sell it and send you the money, give it away, or are you coming back?"

I tried to remember the furniture, what it looked like. Did I want any of it? I didn't want mom's clothes. I wished there were some way Geri could send me some of my clothes. "I don't know. Thanks, though." I was confused. "I'll let you know."

"Well, it's all in our basement."

"Listen. Is anyone after me? I mean, you know, like, the welfare people looking for me—to bring me back?"

I could almost see Geri shrug over the phone. "I don't know. Maybe. I don't know how they handle runaways like you. The foster people probably let the police know just in case you show up in trouble." Then she added in her usual sarcastic way, "Or dead."

"Have your mom or dad said anything about people looking for me?"

"Not that I know of. Why? You do something wrong?"

"Not little ol' me," I tried to joke. "Never fear, Jay is here, remember?" I used to say that whenever Geri worried about some mess we were in. Not that she ever believed me.

"Yeah, right!" she said, accusing me. "Be serious."

"No. Honest. I promise I haven't done nothing wrong." I wanted to tell her about my latest adventure, LT's taking King MacArthur's money and other stuff, but I didn't.

"You should come home, Jay, and you know it," she said. Then added, "I miss you." I knew she meant it, because it wasn't easy for Geri to say things like that. She liked to act tougher than she is.

LT started eyeing me and mouthing the words, "Let's go."

I nodded. "Listen, Geri, I gotta go. Tell Randall hello for me, okay? I'll call you again sometime."

"You'd better, or I'll come after you," she said in her tough voice.

We said goodbye, and as I hung up I could hear her yelling, "Come home, creep!"

At that moment, I wouldn't have minded. But instead I said to LT, "Where're we going?"

# CHAPTER 20

A FTER TALKING with Geri, that dreaded homesick feeling invaded me again. I told myself I didn't have a home anymore, so I shouldn't feel that way now. But I did. I missed Geri. I missed what once was. Silly, I know. So I decided I needed to think of myself as a train gaining speed and couldn't stop until I got where I was going.

"Didn't mean to rush ya' but we don't want to miss our train," LT said, grinning.

Right, like we were running on a time schedule. "Back to the rail yard?" I asked.

"First things first." He pointed to a service station with a mini mart.

Knowing we didn't have to scrounge around in dumpsters set us loose on a buying spree. Ding-Dongs. Honey peanuts. Pretzels. Potato chips. Sliced ham. Bologna. Some yellow cheeses. Bread. Peanut butter and jelly. Donuts. Soda, and I don't remember what all. Even after all that, LT still had some money left.

We divided the stuff according to weight and size. But we had so much it didn't fit in our packs. We each had to carry a full plastic bag. At least we didn't have to worry about eating for a while.

It took about half an hour to make our way back to the tracks. That homesick feeling kept coming and going. The sun had gone down, but the sky still held enough light for us to make our way along a line of rail cars. All the boxcars were shut up and there seemed to be nothing but rows of tanker cars and hoppers full of coal. The train must have been over a mile long. Three diesels were hooked to it.

After waiting with no luck, we crossed the tracks to another row of cars. Another long one. We walked past car after car looking for a good ride. It got dark quickly and we still hadn't found anything to board.

We must have walked another half mile along the train before we came across three or four flatcars. One carried truck trailers full of new BMW X5s. LT let out a small excited, "Yes!"

He dropped his pack and groceries and climbed up on one of the trailers. He tried opening a couple of the cars' doors, but they were locked.

"Toss me my pack," he called down.

I did and watched as he went through it. He pulled out the tool he'd taken from the King. I don't know how he did it, but he managed to open a car door. The light inside the car popped on and LT quickly shut the door. We both looked up and down the train hoping no one saw the light.

I handed the grocery bags and my pack up to LT, then climbed up. We weren't just hopping a train illegally. Now we were breaking and entering an expensive BMW X5. I felt an exciting fear. Riding in a brand new expensive automobile sounded a lot more comfortable than anything I'd ridden so far.

LT opened the car door again and pushed in the little button that turns the light on when the door opens. He held it down while I put all our stuff in the car, then shut the door. I sat in the passenger seat and LT in the driver's. We fooled around adjusting the seats every which way. I made mine go as far back and down as it could. It felt good to stretch out on the leather seat. It was firm and soft at the same time. The new-car smell made me feel rich.

LT sat there holding on to the steering wheel dreaming he was driving. When the thrill was gone, he climbed into the back so he'd have more room. I was fine where I was.

"Wonder where the train's headed?" I hoped it wasn't back toward Chicago.

"Should say on that paper taped on the window where the car's being delivered. Can you read it?"

I tried but it was too dark. Besides, the print was backward from the inside.

"Well, we'll know in the morning," LT said. "Want anything to eat?"

I didn't, but LT must have been hungry. I heard him opening up something. We fell quiet. My mind started going over everything that had happened since morning: the sheriff, the woman on the train, the King of Medals, my phone call to Geri. My mom. I looked at her picture I'd put in my pocket, then put it away.

I tried not to think too much about her, or Geri, so I tried to imagine the real story behind King MacArthur and after many possibilities fell asleep.

The next thing I knew it was getting light out.

LT was already awake. "You're in luck, buddy-boy. We're headin' for Kansas City and points west."

That was good news to me. "How do you know?"

He pointed to the sticker on the BMW's window.

I asked him, "Weren't you headed for Chicago when we met?" I tried to stretch my cramped legs.

"Yeah, well, no hurry."

It flashed through my mind that maybe he was lonely and enjoyed showing me around.

He reached over the seat holding out a bag of potato chips he had opened. "You hungry?"

Still half asleep, I reached in for a handful. I'd never started my day with potato chips before. But so what, I thought. Who made the rules about what to eat at meal time? I was my own boss now.

We finished off the bag, then went for the Ding-Dongs and soda.

"Listen," LT said, "we gotta be careful now that it's light. Someone for sure is gonna check out all the train cars before we pull out of the yard."

"Right." I didn't know what else to say. I worried we might get caught and kicked off, or worse. I just hoped LT had a plan.

"I gotta pee pretty bad," LT said. "You keep your eye out on the left. I'm going to slip out on the right. Keep your head down as much as possible. When I'm through, I'll look out for you."

LT peeked out the window, then slipped out the door and disappeared. When he finished, I did the same.

Back in the BMW I asked, "How can we hide in here when they come lookin'?"

"Can't, unless they're really sloppy. We'll have to get off until after they check, then get back on."

Just then, we got tossed backward as the train gave a slight jolt.

"Yo! This is it, buddy. The train is hookin' up with some cars, then it'll be pulling out. Grab your stuff and let's make it over behind the train on the other tracks."

We looked out the BMW to make sure no one was coming down the tracks checking the load. Not seeing anyone, we jumped down and ran behind a tanker.

LT kept watch on one side of the parked train we hid behind and me the other. Plus, we had to keep an eye on the train with the BMWs. LT warned me to stay and look under the train for feet that might be checking for riders like us. He felt sure there would be someone checking out the cargo. I liked the idea of traveling in a BMW, but I didn't want to get caught at it. The thought put worms burrowing around in my stomach.

Sure enough, LT called it. Peeking under the train, we saw two pair of feet walking along the train. When they got to the flatcar with the BMWs, one pair of the feet disappeared. We knew the rest of the body had climbed up to look inside the cars. If I'd been traveling by myself, I probably would have stayed in the BMW and gotten caught.

We watched as the feet moved on down the train, still checking at our backs. Antsy, I waited for LT to make the first move.

But the first move was by the train we were hiding behind. Instinct had us both jump back as the train moved forward a few feet, then backward. How were we going to get through to our train when our hiding place was moving?

We had to get on the other side of the moving train—and fast. After that first jolt, the metal wheels ground hard against the steel track. That, plus the racket of the couplings clanging into each other as the train moved backward shook me up. I thought about what would happen if I got a foot caught between the hoses and steel connections.

"Make a run for it," LT yelled above the noise.

I hesitated. It meant I had to jump a car, stand on the wobbly coupling between cars, then jump off on the other side.

"Go, before it's too late, "LT warned.

I slipped my pack on my back and grabbed the ladder at the end of one of the cars. Then I swung around putting one foot on the unsteady coupling, still holding a ladder rung. Once my foot felt solidly placed, I swung the other foot around. The coupling swayed back and forth. I tried to balance myself as I turned around so I could jump. It was what I imagined surfing would be like. Except there was no water to fall into, just rocks and gravel.

The train was picking up speed, so I had to jump or stay on. I jumped.

Unsteady, I managed to land on my feet and kept running along with the train for a few feet. I didn't fall, which surprised me, especially with a heavy pack. Maybe I was learning after all. It made me feel good about myself for a change.

I looked back to see how LT was doing.

Man, I wish I hadn't.

# CHAPTER 21

**I** TURNED IN TIME to see what I'll never get out of my mind as long as I live. Either LT slipped or his foot got caught in the coupling. I'll never know. Before I could believe it, his silent body fell, caught between the moving freight cars. Stunned, I watched him being yanked and bumped away like a straw man as the train picked up speed. I fought to accept it was LT. Then I think I yelled, "No!" I'm not sure. I know my brain seemed stuck with the word as he was dragged along.

I stood there, frozen until the train had gone. Then the silence jolted me, and it all became too real. This wasn't Fry Pan telling us about Conductor. I didn't know what to do. I knew I should tell someone, do something. But tell who? And do what? I didn't want to believe it. I just stood there, wanting LT to come up to me and say, "Let's go, Tripper."

I looked down the other track and saw the two men, way down now, still inspecting the train cars. I wanted to do something. I started to call them, but I stopped, worried about what they'd do to me. Anyway, what could they do about LT? His body was probably a mile away by now. Some one would find him, do something. I wanted to believe it.

Maybe it was cold and wrong of me to think of myself, but I guess a survival instinct took over. Keep out of sight. Get back to the BMW. No LT to rely on now.

The thought tightened my throat.

The trailer rack of BMWs was now up the tracks from where I'd jumped the moving train. Watching to make sure the men weren't looking, I climbed over the coupling between two cars so I'd be on the other side of the train from them. I prayed the train wouldn't move while I scooted over. I knew it was dangerous, but it didn't matter. At one point my pack got hooked on a handle and wouldn't come loose. Maybe that's what happened to LT. The heat of panic rushed through me, worried the train might start up. I didn't stop to see how it was caught. Instead, I tugged with all my might and ripped loose one of the pack flaps.

Once on the other side, I made my way back to the X5 and climbed in the back. I didn't know what else to do. I was still too shaken to do any clear thinking. I kept feeling it was what LT would do.

As I slipped off my backpack, I realized I'd left my bag of food where we'd been hiding. Then it really hit me. I'd lost more than a bag of food. I'd lost my friend.

I scootched down on the back seat floor of the BMW. My body started shaking and wouldn't stop. I felt like I should have done something about LT, still wanted to. But I didn't know what.

I couldn't shake off the image of him being dragged under the train. I found myself getting angry with him. He's the one who told me never to do what he did. Look at what it got him.

You were stupid LT.

Then I felt guilty. If he hadn't stuck around to help me, it wouldn't have happened. He'd be in Chicago instead, alive. But I was glad it wasn't me, and that made me feel guilty, too. It could have been me. I was sorry about LT, but glad it wasn't me. It could have been me. It could have been me. It could have been . . .

But it wasn't.

I felt tears forming. I was safe. LT was dead. But I remembered my promise not to ever cry and fought hard to hold it back.

But not for long. I couldn't help it. The tears poured out of me. The more I cried, the more anger I felt. At myself for crying. At my dad and mom for dying and leaving me alone. At LT for leaving me alone. At the world for being so hard on me. At things that didn't even make sense.

My body tightened and my stomach wanted to get out. I had to puke. I barely got the door open before I leaned out and retched out my guts. At that moment, I couldn't have cared less if someone saw me. I might even have welcomed it.

How much time passed before I realized the train was moving, I don't know. I held myself like a baby, too numb to think, but able to feel much more than I wanted. Throwing up left a sour taste in my mouth and my stomach muscles sore.

Thankfully, the train's movements cradled me to sleep and gave me a rest from reality.

I don't know how much later, something caused me to wake up. It was light out.

The front door of the BMW opened a crack. I didn't see anyone at first. Then a head popped up. Then down. Then up, staring at me.

For a split second, I thought it was LT playing with me. I sat up, excited, ready to laugh at my silly mistake.

It wasn't LT.

"Dammit, kid, you scared me near to death," the squinting face said. He turned his body, leaning over the front seat to face me.

His dark hair was cut short, his beard trimmed. I'm not good at guessing ages, but he looked middle-aged. He put some plastic rimmed glasses on.

"That's better." He smiled, looking me over.

I stared back, not smiling. I didn't like him getting in my BMW. I wasn't ready to be friendly. I wanted him to be LT.

"Sorry to intrude," he said, still smiling, "but this was the only unlocked car on the transport. You found it first, so by rights it's yours. Rules of the road, yeah? Should I leave, or is it okay with you if I stay aboard?"

I shrugged. What was with the polite talk? Rules of the road? What was I supposed to do, tell him to get out? Even if I did, would he leave?

"Does that shrug mean yes or no?"

I shrugged again. "Don't care." My voice cracked, dry from all the crying. I didn't want to sound weak to a stranger.

"Thanks. Appreciate it. Riding in here beats rockin' in a hopper." He turned around and started going through his pack. After a moment, he turned back to me and held out an orange.

"Want one?" he asked.

I shook my head.

He began to peel the orange. "Don't talk much, do you? Just as well. I'm a reader myself. You a reader?"

I shook my head. After what I'd seen happen to LT, I didn't feel like talking. I just wanted to be still with my mixed-up feelings and thoughts.

"Sorry, not trying to be nosey, just friendly. It's a long ride to Kansas."

He turned around and slid over to the passenger seat. He put the orange peelings in a plastic bag, then dampened a handkerchief or something with some water and wiped off his fingers. He asked if he could move the seat back some and I nodded. He took a book from his pack and started reading.

I looked out the window, not paying much attention to what went by. It didn't seem right there was no family or someone who should be told about LT. I didn't know his real name or where he came from. I didn't know why he even became a hobo. Four years he said he'd been riding freights. He'd been so sure of himself. Now he was gone.

I don't know how much time went by like that, me silent, the man making a few snorts and laughs as he read. At one point, he said, "Oh, listen to this. This is great." He read something from the book and laughed. "Funny, huh?" he said, not turning around.

I didn't listen, just stared out the window.

We stayed in our spaces like that for a while, which was fine with me. Then he slapped his book shut.

"Say, I have a book here you might like to read." He went through his backpack and handed me a book. "Ever read this one? Maybe you've seen the movie."

I read the title of the beat-up paperback: *The Outsiders*. I'd never heard of it. The book cover showed a bunch of teenage guys trying to look cool.

"It's a classic. You'll like it."

"Why?" My voice sounded gruff. I didn't mean to speak aloud, but I didn't feel like talking about books.

But the guy couldn't seem to stop talking. "The author, S. E. Hinton? She wrote the book when she was a teenager. Sixteen, I think. She used her initials because she didn't think any publisher would take on a book written by a teenage girl. Funny, huh? Now, years later, it's a classic young adult book."

I just looked at him. I could see he was trying to be friendly, but I wasn't in the mood.

"See," he went on, pointing at the back of the book cover, "the summary tells you what the book's about. Yeah, a fourteen-year-old boy named Ponyboy whose parents had died. His loyalty to his brother and his gang from the wrong side of the tracks gets him involved in a lot of trouble."

"I've got enough troubles of my own," I said. "I don't need to read about someone else's." I wasn't sure if it was me or LT talking.

He dropped his smile. "Yeah, sure. Sorry. I get carried away sometimes. Just thought you might like to read the book to pass the time. It's a good one for young guys like you."

"You don't even know me," I barked back. I don't know why I was so angry with him. Maybe because he was being too nice, and I couldn't take it. Maybe because I didn't like him thinking he knew so much. Maybe because I didn't trust him. Anger just seemed to have filled me up.

"True," he answered, "I don't know your name. But I'll bet I know more than you think. You're fifteen-sixteen or so. Under age, anyway. I'll bet you're a runaway, maybe parentless, no happy family anyway. I'll bet you think if you get away from home things will get better. You've no money and no real future plans. I'll bet you're scared . . ."

"I'm not scared," I shot back. "And my plan is to go to California." I couldn't help wondering if I sounded as experienced as LT. LT would know how to talk to this guy.

"Okay, I'll give you that, but I'm right about the other things, aren't I?"

I didn't look at him. Out the BMW's window everything was flashing by. Trees. Buildings. Telephone poles. Fields. Street lamps. Cars. Nothing stayed in sight very long.

LT was dead. My mind saw it happen again. It could have been me. Still could be me.

"My friend just died." I guess I needed to say it out loud. "Got dragged under a train back there."

"You saw it?"

I nodded.

"Sheez, boy, I'm really sorry. That's a tough one to take." He sounded sincere.

I told him how it happened, how I wanted to help but couldn't. It just poured out.

He was quiet for a minute. Then he said, "Yeah, it's dangerous jumpin' trains."

"You do it."

He nodded. "Guess that's part of the attraction. There's a thrill to it, I admit. But it doesn't make it right or safe. I could pay my way, but I like the challenge. But I'm cautious. I plan ahead. I know how to get where I'm going and how to get back. It's become a summer hobby with some of us. Still, it's illegal, and I say all this to rationalize what I do, knowin' it's wrong."

He shut up after that and turned back to his book. I needed to get my mind off LT, but I couldn't.

# CHAPTER 22

M Y EYES FELL on the book he'd left on the seat beside me. It was hard to believe a sixteen-year-old girl could write a book that would become famous. If what he said was even true. I wondered if I could ever write what's been happening to me. Probably not. Would people believe in characters like Hopper Bill, Fry Pan, the woman on the train, or Liberty Two?

I handed the book back. "Here. Thanks."

"Don't you want to read it?"

"Naw. I need to travel light." A stupid thing to say. It didn't take up that much space. It would have been a good thing to read sometime.

"Go on, keep it," he said, shoving the book back to me. "I need to lighten my load. Got too many books here."

I shrugged and took it. I should have said thanks, but it didn't come out.

He started going through his pack and pulling out a brown bag. "I'm starving. Want some apple slices and cheese?"

"Not really hungry," I said in truth. My stomach still felt queasy.

He cut some apple slices and cheese and handed them to me. "Best eat, son. I know you're grieving and all, but you're alive and your friend isn't. Be respectful and eat."

I didn't know what he meant about being respectful, but I didn't feel like arguing, so I chewed on a few bites, not really tasting it.

He started up again. "I've been doing summer train riding off and on for several years now. Met some interesting riders. A few like you." He smiled while he chewed. "Some not so nice. How long have you been riding?"

I didn't see any harm in telling him. "Not long."

He nodded. "Your friend you lost. Did you know him well?"

I found myself saying more than I'd intended about myself. But it felt good to talk about it to someone. I told him how I'd met LT, how he'd helped me, everything that had happened.

He handed me some more apple slices and cheese. "Sad business. But don't you feel guilty. There's nothing you could have done. I know it sounds callous, but what happened to your friend happens too often on these freights. Did you know, last year, over five hundred people were killed and hundreds injured trespassing on trains or on railroad property? It gets worse every year. It's dangerous."

"Then why d'you do it?" I asked.

"Good question." He offered me a small bottle of lemonade. I shook my head and drank from my own bottle of water.

"At first it was the rush of the ride, the danger, the challenge. It's so different from office work. And I'd read a lot about famous writers who've ridden freights at one time or another. Walt Whitman, Mark Twain, Jack Kerouac, Ralph Ellison. Anyway, I thought maybe I could get a book out of my adventures, so I keep a journal." He pulled a book from his pack and flipped the pages filled with notes and drawings.

He went on. "I'm makin' this my last summer to ride. I've seen enough. I'm on my way home. The romance is gone, so to speak, so I'm foldin' my hand. Besides, I'm somewhat of a fake. I don't need to run away. I have a job I like. I could pay my way. And I guess I know more and have more sense now. I don't want to end up like your friend, or be one of the eight thousand riders arrested every year."

I'd been sort of arrested, but I didn't say anything. What was there to say?

"So, what are you gonna do now?" he asked.

"Make it to California, if I can." As I said it, I wondered if I could do it without LT.

He nodded. "Look, son, it's none of my business, but let me tell you. In the years I've been riding, I've met people who call themselves the 'new-age' hobos, a subculture that uses the Internet to plan journeys. But where does it really get them? I've met runaways, squatters living out of dustbins, gutter punks begging for money. I've seen the violence done by members of the notorious Freight Train Riders Association. Sure, you meet some decent folks, too. Some are just down on their luck, as the saying goes."

I knew where he was heading and didn't really want to hear any more. I let out a deep sigh and hunched back in my seat.

"I know," he went on like he could read my mind, "I'm not saying anything you want to hear. But I'm saying it anyway. Chalk it up to the busybody in me. You think you can take care of yourself. What d'ya think you'll find out west that will make your life any easier? What makes you think you can even make it there? Where would you be now without your dead friend's help?"

If he expected an answer, he didn't get it. I was sorry I'd already told him so much.

"I know you're thinking here's another adult trying to tell you what to do. I'm not telling you what to do. I'm just trying to get you to think through what you're doing and why. If you're determined to go through with your plan, good luck."

He stopped talking and wrote something in his journal. I heard him tear out a page. He turned and handed it to me.

"Here's my name, address and phone number in Kansas City. You're welcome to stay with me until you catch another ride west. Or, you can stay as long as you want, and I'll help you in any way I can. I'll stake you the fare to a train ticket home if you want. So, that's it. No more sermons."

He turned his back to me and stretched out best he could in the front of the X5. He pulled his hat over his face, crossed his arms and gave the impression he was going to sleep.

I looked at the paper he gave me and started to crumple it up. Who did this guy think he was, anyway? Why was he inviting me to stay with him? Maybe he was a pervert. I'd heard about guys that come on real nice and friendly, then try to get you to do weird things.

Then again, maybe he was for real. He seemed sincere, like maybe he did want to help me.

I folded the paper and put it in the shirt pocket with my mom's picture. I looked out the window and saw my reflection. Who was that looking back at me?

A thought mix-master started up.

I didn't like it, but he was right. I didn't have any real plan. I was a runaway. I was running away from my mother's death. I was running away from having to learn to live with a foster family. I was running away from my old friends, like Geri and Randall. I was running away from Allonia, the place I'd called home all my life.

I was running away, but what was I running *to*? I didn't know anyone in California. I didn't even know what put the idea in my brain in the first place. Getting there hadn't been easy so far. Things could get a lot harder from now on.

I needed to get my head straight and decide what I really wanted to do.

This guy's invitation to stay with him—that was an option. Was he as real as he sounded? It would be a gamble. What would he expect from me in return? But if I stayed with him for a while, I could take more time to decide whether or not I want to continue on to California. And he offered to stake me to a ticket back home.

Going back home would mean living with a foster family. Could I do it? I remembered what Geri had said on the phone about the people who wanted me. Her parents said they were okay. Geri's parents were cool; they wouldn't lie. So, I had that option if I wanted to go back.

And I really missed Geri. Even Randall. Two true friends. And I ran away from them, too.

My mind couldn't focus on anything very long, too much to think about. And while I tried to makes sense of it all, I swear the clicking sound of the rolling train wheels seemed to say, "Go back home—go back home—go back home, Jay . . ."